DAN BROTZEL'S short story collection, *Hotel du Jack*, was published in 2020. His stories have appeared widely in literary magazines and journals, and have won or been short-listed for several awards. He is also co-author of a comic novel-in-emails about an eccentric writers' group, *Work in Progress* (Unbound). He lives in London with his family.

THE
WOLF
IN THE
WOODS

DAN BROTZEL

SANDSTONE PRESS

First published in Great Britain in 2021 by
Sandstone Press Ltd
PO Box 41
Muir of Ord
IV6 7YX
Scotland

www.sandstonepress.com

ISBN: 978-1-913207-62-5
ISBNe: 978-1-913207-63-2

The Author and Publisher are grateful to Lloyd Cole
for kind permission to quote part of the lyric for
Four Flights Up by Lloyd Cole and the Commotions.

Sandstone Press is committed to a sustainable future.
This book is made from Forest Stewardship Council ® certified paper.

For Rob

This fellow is wise enough to play the fool

William Shakespeare, Twelfth Night

Oh, must you tell me all your secrets
When it's hard enough to love you knowing nothing?

Lloyd Cole and the Commotions, 'Four Flights Up'

SATURDAY

Oh God. Here you go again, hanging over me, invading my sleep with your morning breath. As my eyes flicker open, you hang over me for a long moment, nuzzling my neck and furtively assessing my reaction. I feel your arms tremble.

When you get no response, you slide off with a disgusted grunt. Even though I'm still half-asleep, I sense the guilt-seeking rays emanating from your half-turned back. I roll over and away.

But you just can't let me be, can you? The pointed buzzing of an electric toothbrush, the pedantic click of a wardrobe door, a coat-hanger's righteous jangle – your busy-busy faffing is just enough to break my spell. I am conscious, and there's no escaping it. No escaping you.

Today, I think. Let it be today that I find a way.

'Come on!' you say. 'We should have left by now!'

And I think: Next week.

I. ON THE ROAD

'Come on, love, let's get cracking! We should have left by now!'

In his head their car was a Morris Hillman estate, and by his side there was a golden retriever wagging its tail and bouncing up and down, barking with excitement at the adventure to come. There were a couple of delightfully enthusiastic young children laughing and jumping about too, running around with sailboats and kites under their arms as Daddy packed the wicker picnic hamper, tartan blankets and a couple of those retro brown suitcases with the reinforced corners and luggage labels that say things like HOTEL EXCELSIOR – NICE and FABULOUS LAS VEGAS and P&O FIRST CLASS: LONDON – RIO – CAIRO – NEW YORK. [Not a practicable itinerary? Sod that. It was his fantasy.]

His wife, when she emerged, wore a silken headscarf and understated shades. She radiated both maternal benevolence and an exotic carnality that was his, and his alone. She was utterly perfect in every way, and she wanted only him, and he deserved it all.

Back in the real world and out of his head [as he had been last night, a tad], their car was a metallic turquoise Vauxhall Astra estate, there were no children or dogs, and the luggage was the usual random selection of IKEA rucksacks, old vinyl holdalls with split zips, a buckled carry-on, and several Asda carrier bags full of last-minute essentials such as underwear, tampons, paperbacks and coffee: a pack of freeze-dried ground, several boxes of one-cup filters, and [for backup] two jars of nice instant. Also, aspirin.

Jesus, to think they might have left for a cottage stay without coffee or aspirin, like Withnail. But this was always the way with them – the important stuff went in last.

Andrew's head banged painfully with the exertion of packing. His mind was clouded by a post-alcoholic awareness that he had no energy for or interest in packing, and no idea of what to pack. This fuzziness was itself overlaid by a grey tinge of guilt which whispered in his mind's ear that he would no doubt pay later for his crapness on the packing front. But this feeling was in turn smeared with the grimy residue of a further guilty realisation: that he still couldn't really bring himself to give a toss.

On top of all this – or behind, or below all this – there additionally lay a sort of muffled crust of guilty resentment that Colleen had rebuffed his attempts to have sex this morning.

He would probably have felt more upset about this if he could recall the incident fully, or if he had been more invested in the effort, which struck him now as a reflex move powered entirely by the morning's predictable hangover horniness. He was disappointed in himself, because he did in fact want to make love with his wife very much, and [not that anyone was counting] it had been a while. This sort of footling behaviour was unlikely to advance his cause.

'Who's going to feed the cats?' called Colleen from the doorway. The cleaner would be in to do the honours on Monday, but there was no one to hold the fort over the weekend. [Although: had anyone actually mentioned any of this to the cleaner?] Colleen always remembered about the cats, sooner or later, which was much more than he did.

She looked, he thought, like someone famous who's just slipped out of rehab. Dark glasses, hair scraped back. Flowing linen and cotton lines, incidental cleavage he couldn't help admiring, a battered leather handbag that had obviously been expensive once. She wore too-bold lipstick, as she often did at such moments, and her scent – though by no means unpleasant – would, he knew, fill the car with its sharp citrus for many a mile, and keep his throat at the edge of nausea all the way. It was something in the quality of her morning skin that gave her away. It had a scrubbed, pinkish glow, as if she had been trying to scour away the excesses of the night before and then paper them over with foundation or concealer, or whatever the modern lady uses.

Not that he could talk. A while ago, at a client party, a passing acquaintance had complimented him on having 'the ruddy skin of a true outdoorsman'. Andrew didn't have the heart to tell his new pal that he'd been sitting at a computer for the past thirty years. Colleen looked, he supposed, like someone trying to cover up a monstrous hangover. He looked, he supposed, much the same.

No one, it transpired, was going to feed the cats. Or rather they both were. Colleen remembered now that she had left bowls of dry food all around the house, to go with the many saucers and old ashtrays of water which Andrew had earlier filled and spilled in various rooms too. The discovery of this inadvertent yet surprisingly purposeful collaboration briefly delighted them both and was enough to get them into the car, out on the road and away.

In accordance with time-honoured tradition, Andrew opened the gate and guided Colleen out; though she was a much better driver than him, she hated reversing. But she would drive first, she always did.

As Colleen reversed, Andrew quietly said goodbye to their Edwardian suburban villa, wondering superstitiously if this would be the last time he ever saw its peeling faux-Tudor facade, its stone cats, its low-maintenance front beds. 'Nothing ever flowers in our garden!' Colleen had often complained. 'That's because we never put anything in those beds that actually flowers,' said Andrew. To which Colleen would reply: 'Well, when was the last time you planted *anything*?' This argument had a cyclical quality to it, like a gardener's calendar.

Houses and cars have faces, Andrew believed, and his house had long worn the generous welcoming smile of a capacious family home, overflowing with benevolent bustle and delighted clutter. Back in the day, its pretty little patterned windows seemed to wink and beam at them in the distance as they went [*wended?*] their weary way back, laden with buggies and scooters, from yet another trip to the playground or the ducks or the local woods.

But as the children had grown up and left, so the house had started to let itself go.

From a distance it was still a pretty enough residence in a broadly desirable area. But look a little closer, and there were touches everywhere of middle-aged spread: wrinkles in the paintwork and stretch-marks in the walls, creaking joints and falling arches, receding sightlines and paunchy plasterwork.

Now that they were leaving, Andrew saw his surroundings as if for the first time. That funny house on the corner that looked like a ski chalet. The fancy one opposite with the wrought-iron violins in its grand gates. The one two streets down with the OTT security, the odd sculptures in the garden and the general air of secrecy – the one that everyone said was the home of a disgraced diplomat in hiding from his rogue government, or else the HQ of a clandestine cult.

Or perhaps both? Whenever he drove past, Andrew looked closely at the mystery house for clues. But no one was ever to be seen coming in or out, and his curiosity found no answer. This situation reminded him of the opening pages of *The Voyages of Doctor Dolittle*, in which Tommy, the narrator, recalls the first time he finally met the famous animal-doctor.

Dreaming of the sea and desperate to meet the mythical man he's heard so much about, little Tommy takes to walking out day after day to the doctor's house on the edge of their town, Puddleby-on-the-Marsh. But the gate is always locked, because the doctor is still away on one of his voyages. Until one cold, wet day, when Tommy has all but given up hope, he bumps into a friendly elderly man who offers to help him dry off in the warm. Miraculously the man takes him back to the silent house and unlocks the gates – for it is none other than Doctor Dolittle himself.

Remembering his first encounter with this fictional moment as a child – the little boy's endless wait, his daily fruitless pilgrimage, the beckoning ocean, the ever-locked gates, the extraordinary serendipity of the doctor's appearance – Andrew realised that this was probably the moment that he first knew books would always seem more real to him than life. [He'd read the passage out to Colleen once, in the early days. She was more worried about the implications of a little boy being taken into a mysterious house by a strange old man.]

Back on the road, Andrew was suddenly fascinated by the variety of vans on display at his local Volkswagen Commercial Vehicle Centre, admiring the deft way they were all wedged in at tight, precarious angles atop the fake little display hillocks that surrounded the showroom.

As a rule, Andrew liked steering things. When the children were small he was happy to relive some of the steering challenges of his childhood, like manoeuvring a toy lorry in and out of a Lego slalom of Ned's devising, or guiding a remote-control boat through one of those little model waterscapes, rounding lighthouses and threading tight rocky arches. In another life, he might have enjoyed a job where the main requirement was to be able to park things in tight spaces, a bit like Dean Moriarty in *On the Road*, 'the most fantastic parking-lot attendant in the world', who could reverse a car into a tight spot at 40mph and jump into the next one before the driver had even got out – 'leap literally under him as he steps out'. Andrew admired extreme dexterity, especially in small things.

Now Colleen was driving them past a local gas-holder frame, and Andrew was suddenly moved by this giant Victorian cylindrical trellis, with its intricate latticed guide-rails and cast-iron columns surmounted by capitals of a quite unnecessary neo-classical elegance [Doric, was it?]. Far more work had gone in than was functionally necessary, and there was something beautiful about this excess of creativity. Andrew was a notorious weeper at the best of times, a man who could be moved to tears by the euphoria of a winning couple on *Pointless*, or the crude storyline of a car insurance ad involving a confused toddler and a willing puppy. [As for *DIY SOS*, even the theme tune got him going.] And now he felt a lump at the thought of all the care that had gone into the making of these gas holders, and how they were being removed from our skylines for ever, or else transformed into ironic monuments to a later generation's inability to remember its own past, or somesuch thing. [Good word, *somesuch*.]

They drove past a small fleet of parked ice-cream vans, a giant cemetery and a sprawling allotment, these last two looking oddly similar to Andrew's bleary eye. In the distance, a famous radio mast on a hill. Colleen clenched the wheel grimly. *Any Questions?* was on, and already she was tutting violently at a Tory grandee who was putting a boldly complacent face on what the previous speaker, an up-and-coming Labour firebrand, had just labelled 'the worst economic figures in living memory'.

He envied Colleen in this moment; she knew exactly what she thought. Andrew, on the other hand, could be swayed by anyone. Though instinctively he distrusted any Tory on tribal north-London grounds, this particular man spoke rather beautifully, he thought, his mild Scottish lilt dancing agreeably along resonant, sophisticated sentences. This was not a man afraid to use expressions like 'outwith' and 'shrill' and 'trespassing on your listeners' patience'.

Andrew liked words and sentences, especially as things in themselves. He liked to pick one up and roll it around in his mind, as if he'd never heard it before, and then he liked to think about its etymology, or imagine how best to translate it into French or German or Spanish or Italian. Or even Latin, at a pinch.

Scanning his mental innards, Andrew knew it would be at least a couple of hours before roads and vehicles and central reservation barriers seemed at all real to him, rather than the mere furniture of some shaky virtual cityscape, and he knew – albeit as an intellectual fact rather than a lived truth – that it was not ideal to be driving when your mind was tempted by thought experiments about impact and collision and *Is reality really real?* and *What would really happen if I drove into that oncoming lorry?*

Andrew liked to believe that Colleen didn't think such things, and didn't know that he did; that she just liked driving first. But the truth was, he had never dared ask her.

II. DEALING WITH DIFFICULT PEOPLE

After the fifth missed call of the drive, Colleen finally gave in.

'Do you have to?' he asked, still not sure if he was ready to drive.

'At £175 an hour, *yes, I do.*'

They stopped at the next service station. Andrew went to get coffees, while Colleen went off to do her call. Though she was not a therapist technically, or at all, she said she couldn't speak in the car as it would be inappropriate for Andrew to listen in. Also, the client would be able to tell if she wasn't alone, which would *undermine the dynamic.* This, of course, as she hoped he understood, was just a fancy way of saying that they could probably both do with a moment's space from each other.

Although she described her company as a 'communications consultancy', which ran workshops for businesses in things like media training, effective presentation skills, dealing with difficult people and motivating your team, Colleen's main work these days was as a one-to-one coach.

Allegedly she advised big hitters on communicating more effectively, influencing stakeholders, maximising their impact in the boardroom and so on. But once she got them alone, they took one look at her wise kind face, sensed her frank emotional intelligence, possibly also sized up her ample maternal bosom (this was mostly pale, stale males we were talking about), and started pouring their lives out – their hopes, their fears, their secrets, their regrets.

I confess. Senior executives notorious for their corporate ruthlessness would sob to Colleen about the wives who didn't understand them, the mistresses who wanted too much and the childhood traumas they had never gotten over. Ice-cold asset-strippers agonised about errant children. Disgustingly perfect power-dressers admitted to crippling fear and envy. Heartless money men confessed their insider-trading; family-first heads of department came out to her.

Colleen knew who was about to get fired, who was sleeping with who, who was about to file for divorce – often before the other party did. On one occasion, she had sessions on con-secutive days, first with a woman who confessed to cheating on her boring husband, and then with the actual husband, who was plagued with chronic insomnia and a strange, persist-ent sensation that the ground was falling away beneath his feet. *Thank God for my amazing wife*, he said, *she's my absolute rock. But what can I do about the other stuff?*

Try harder. Look closer. Lawyer up. These were just a few of the things that Colleen did not say. She was like a priest carrying around the secrets of her confessional – though occasionally she did try a few out on Andrew, in heavily anonymised form. (Andrew liked to joke that he and Colleen had met professionally, which did make her chuckle – the first few times he said it, anyway.)

At first, Colleen felt uneasy about her work. These people told her so much, made themselves so vulnerable, needed real help sometimes, and she had no clinical training or formal mental-health skills. She cared about them, and she wanted to help, but was she really qualified? True, she was a skilled active listener and a trained actor, and she was not afraid or embarrassed by other people's problems, all of which got you a long way. She had toyed with the idea of doing a counselling qualification on the quiet, just for her own reassurance, but the fact was that these alpha players would never be seen dead in any kind of therapeutic or clinical setting. Admitting to seeing a psychiatrist or needing counselling would be an unthinkable humiliation to people who traded millions on the back of a confident hunch, and who always had to project an aura of peak performance.

But that pressure has to find an outlet somewhere, and someone like Colleen was perfect. She came in under the guise of something perfectly innocent-sounding like 'performance coach' or 'sales consultant', ostensibly there just to hone someone's vocal delivery or help them rehearse for an important pitch. But then, once the door was closed and rapport established, the client had no qualms dumping whatever crap they were carrying around – inadequacy, jealousy, rage; guilt, despair, anxiety, fear . . . you name it.

In the early days, Colleen would try and come up with answers for the problems she accidentally uncovered. She read up about self-esteem and the formation of the personality, about the major schools of psychotherapy and the self-help shortcuts of CBT. But she soon realised that no one was looking for her to solve anything. They just wanted someone discreet and non-judgemental who could really *listen*. In fact, she found that the less she said, the more powerful people found the sessions.

Sometimes she dared herself to go the whole fifty minutes without saying a word. And invariably, it was at the end of one of these sessions that her client would go furthest in their praise of her 'work'. 'Feck-moi, you've got a gift,' said one. 'I'm gonna tell Gordon about you.' As Gordon was the global CEO of that particular firm, and one of the world's 200 richest individuals, this was praise of a (terrifyingly) high order. 'Please don't,' she wanted to say.

Referrals begat referrals. Once she was on the inside of this world, Colleen found that her details began to whizz silently around high-powered networks, as clients of hers personally recommended her to high-net-worth colleagues and contacts of their own. Having Colleen in your phone was a badge of status, to be wielded or bestowed at a moment of shared confidence, after a third or fourth cocktail.

And of course Colleen was handsomely paid for her discretion. It was embarrassing how much they paid her, really, especially if you thought about what actual health professionals got. Colleen campaigned for the NHS, and supported her local Labour party, but she had also maxed out her ISA several years running, oversaw a decent private pension and was growing a plump little stock portfolio (with some discreet guidance from a client or two).

The ironies of the situation did sometimes give her pause, if she let them. But she couldn't help having a natural gift for something that certain people valued very highly. And then other things would distract her thoughts, like Andrew making one of his not-really-a-joke jokes about how it was incredible that someone who made a living out of listening to other people could have so little empathy or understanding for their own husband. *How is it that you can get yourself in a state like this – yet be seen as this beacon of sanity and well-adjusted wisdom by your clients?* Etc etc. Et bloody cetera.

I'm your private listener, she would sometimes hum to herself as she looked out over the City from another all-glass lift on its way to another penthouse office.

I listen for money, and any old secret will do.

III. SORRY NOT SORRY

Andrew queued for another double *espresso* – not *expresso*, of course, a frequent English usage – another *latte*, two *croissants*, plus a *bruschetta* as a surreptitious little side order for himself, causing no little confusion by insisting on pronouncing the word [bruˈsketta], like the pedantic twat he was, rather than [bɹʊˈʃɛʔɐ], as tends to be the British way. He restrained himself from ordering an unduly pluralised *panino*, a behaviour which always held up queues, but took a moment instead to enjoy his server's pronunciation of *croissant*, which started off with a very nice French [r] but then ended up very Britishly sounding the final consonant.

Andrew didn't judge people for such things; he just liked making a note of the differences and quietly pointing out that there was another way, probably one that was more authentic and which he happened to know about, and some others obviously didn't. Colleen accused him of deliberately only ordering food with phonetically problematic names, so he could take pleasure in correcting serving staff. He felt compelled to do this because he was 'a fetid grammarsplainer', she said – which observation he sort of enjoyed, at least linguistically. [He dared hope that Colleen meant not fetid but *fervid*, though he suspected not; he also couldn't help noting that she pronounced her chosen adjective with a long rather than a short 'e', which he felt always said a lot about a person.]

Through the wall of plate-glass Andrew caught sight of his wife, pacing up and down by some moulded plastic picnic benches in a thin grassy area separating the edge of a lorry park from a small, flooded chalk-pit masquerading as a duck pond. The pond was a crude hole lined with tiers of concrete breeze blocks, their crude moulded surfaces still halfexposed beneath a sort of crude AstroTurf matting. The surrounding rows of young trees still had their spirally plastic sleeves half-on, and the water level in the pond was so low that even the ducks – about half a dozen mallards, straight from central casting – looked vaguely insulted. A persistent dull boom of high-speed traffic washed continuously over the whole scene.

It was, in short, about the last place in the world anyone would want to have a picnic.

Colleen, still on the phone, made a few gestures to him through the glass window, conveying an enormous amount of information with an economy of effort that only two people who've been together for twenty-plus years could ever hope to attain.

Sorry this call is taking so long, she gestured. *Only not sorry, as you know this is my job and this is what it involves sometimes? Also you don't mind the money it makes which, if we're honest, amounts to rather more – and arrives rather more consistently – than the dribbles your so-called translation business brings in. (Or* transcreation *as you insist on calling it.) The weather's nice, though, isn't it? Looks like we've avoided the rain. Give me five more minutes, I reckon. Do you think the cats are OK? Also, did you put sugar in this latte? You know I've given up. And no, I don't want a lecture on the different ways to say* latte, *thanks. Have you just eaten an extra bruschetta by the way? Well, it's your funeral. You know you're probably pre-diabetic. Why do you think I got you that Fitbit?*

Behind her, a mallard stared sceptically out over the edge of the thin water.

Andrew resumed another lap of the service station. He was on 1753 steps for the day, so he might as well try and get his numbers up. He assumed they'd go for a long walk this evening when they got there, perhaps wander over a sandy clifftop path down to a rocky cove, maybe even dip their feet in the glistening emerald sea. It was mid-September, after all, and still agreeably mild. But things with them had a habit of taking longer than planned and, despite her assurances, Colleen's call looked far from over.

IV. TERRY FROM QUIVER

Colleen looked up and saw Andrew standing at the window, head bent over his phone. He was stabbing an awkward finger at his emails, in that infuriating way of his, occasionally glancing round to see if anyone was reading over his shoulder.

Colleen was not actually on the phone to a client at all, not any more. Terry from Quiver Investments had been seeking her advice about his chronic jealousy. After a messy split with his wife of twenty-three years last year – which Colleen had done her best to help him through – Terry had now hooked up with a Croatian glamour model about a third his age. She was everything he ever wanted, but how could he be sure that she really loved him and wasn't just in it for the cash? After all, she was young and beautiful and had it all going for her ('and not just on the outside'), whereas he was fat, fifty-seven and rich, 'and that's about it'. (Well, quite.) Every time Basia got on her phone or started looking at her iPad, he worried, was she chatting to an ex or flirting with some footballer who was trying to tune into her?

Very good questions, Tel, you sad self-deluded gammon was what Colleen always remembered not to say, as instead she made appreciative grunts and conciliatory humming noises down the phone. She was just thumbing through her mental card index of advanced platitudes – something about 'the attraction of opposites', perhaps? – when Terry suddenly announced that Basia had finished exfoliating and was now going in for a tan – which gave him a good thirty minutes, he said, to check through her search history and install a couple of bits on spyware.

'Cheers, Colleen, babe,' said Terry, signing off. 'You've only gone and done it again.'

It was amazing, this capacity she had, to make other people feel better who didn't deserve to. And to achieve it by not really doing anything.

She was about to go and join Andrew in the coffee queue when another call came in. Not a client, this time, but her own unresolved case: Gerry.

V. ANAL TEARING

As Andrew tinkled away unconvincingly into a small cluster of wee-drenched little cubes, he examined the poster before his eyes. It bore a picture of three men in a row, each naked except for a bush hat covering their genitals. Two of the men had to hold on to their hats, but the third – significantly, Andrew noted, neither the youngest nor the buffest – was standing proud, with both hands behind his head. The head-line: 'Guess who's used our online doctor?' Geddit? His enormous stork was obviously doing the heavy lifting.

Andrew looked around for more messages. On the same theme, he found: 'Go online. It's not hard.' He also found: 'Pain in the ar*e? Repair your tear.' 'Having a drink could cost more than you think.' 'It's what you'd call a van's van.' Also: 'At last – a cremation plan that needn't cost the earth.'

Andrew loved the blokeish intimacy of service-station loos, which had a gratifyingly direct way of talking to men – *entre nous*, fellas – about the stuff that really matters. Stuff that men don't get much of a chance to discuss elsewhere, like anal fissures, alcoholism and erectile dysfunction. Everything gets the toilet treatment, whether it's your mobile package ['a steady stream of talk and text'] or a global humanitarian crisis ['FLUSH POVERTY AWAY'].

Death. Vans. My bum hurts. I can't get it up. How much data do you get with that? All man-life is here, all the big questions. And there's no need to be worried about any of it, guys, because there's a toilet pun for everything. No need to worry about squat.

The drink-making-you-think one caught his eye again. From somewhere in the subterranean recesses of his mind, a

15

dark, unthinkable thought bubbled up to the surface of a rockpool in his consciousness and expired with a dull pop, releasing a noxious half-memory of a distant half-pledge. Did he . . . ? Had they really . . . ? All week? Surely not all week? But at least . . . Oh, Lordy Lord.

An email popped up that really shouldn't have. He forwarded it somewhere safe, and deleted it fast, looking around him nervously as he did so, like a crap spy.

VI. THE WORLD ON A STICK

Gerry was always a handsome bastard, and he knew it. But it wasn't really his beauty that everyone gravitated to – drama school was full of dramatic-looking young blokes who weren't afraid to show off their assets, same as the women. No, the thing about Gerry was his extraordinary theatrical presence.

Gerry had first attracted Colleen's attention when she'd seen him performing at an end-of-term production of *Twelfth Night*, in drama school. Gerry was playing Sir Toby Belch, the pisshead uncle and nominal head of grief-struck Olivia's household. It's a relatively minor and straightforwardly comic part, that of a man who stands up for noisy good cheer and laddish bantz in a play where everyone else is in the grips of a modish, indulgent melancholy. But he played it with such flair and aplomb and elan, with a sort of insouciant bravado that channelled the spirits of Rik Mayall, Ollie Reed and Sergeant Wilson all rolled into one, plus some magical extra ingredient all his own, that when he wasn't on stage, Colleen – and, she had no doubt, the rest of the audience – yearned for his reappearance.

Certain of Sir Toby's phrases, with Gerry's intonations and rhythms, had stayed with her down the years. 'These clothes are good enough to drink in.' 'Oh knight! Thou lackest a cup of canary.' That was a line she and Andrew still used to cheer each other on sometimes. And when the kids were little, if one of them was up to no good, she'd say, 'I smell a device!'

A few years later, when Colleen was in rep and trying to write her own stuff, she'd got to know a few agents. She remembered asking one of them – a former star of very British farces who still bore the face of a naughty schoolboy, albeit now with a voluminous grey beard covering a massive treble chin – what it was he looked for when he sat talent-scouting at the back of a drama school performance or a provincial first night.

'It's simple, darling,' he said. 'You just look for the one that no one can take their eyes off.'

The answer had offended her at the time. What about craft and technique? Raw emotion allied to actorly *intelligence*? But every time she recalled the agent's words over the years, she found that she agreed with him more and more. Life was unfair, but some people simply had charisma and others didn't. For all the money her boardroom sharks spent on trying to *maximise their personal impact*, the truth was that no amount of money could buy the sort of magnetic power that Gerry effortlessly commanded.

Gerry made you want to be a better version of yourself. The light of the cosmos appeared to shine through his eyes. If he looked your way in a rehearsal or down the pub, you felt instantly blessed, *chosen*. You might also want to sleep with him or be his best friend or be cast in his next production, but that was just incidental. She and Gerry had had their moments, but then Gerry had his moments with just about everyone, of both sexes, often a few at a time allegedly – seemingly just to keep up with demand. This was drama school, after all, where snogging practice was on the syllabus.

After graduating, Gerry encouraged Colleen to keep writing, and even put on one of her plays – a two-hander about race and gender and the evils of Thatcherism, as most things were in those days. The piece had run for six full nights in a small theatre above a pub in south London. It had been seen by about sixty people in all, most of them friends and relatives of either Colleen or the other actor. After each performance the audience would split into two even smaller factions, and sit at opposite ends of the pub, loudly bigging up the performance of their own favourite and bitching about the other. Colleen's one review – in a local listings sheet – had focused on the deplorable lack of real ale behind the bar.

And yet she had loved every single moment. Dressing the set, learning the lines, printing the flyers. The agony of nerves. The thrill of performance. The naked irreversible *fuck-it*-ness of being *live.* 'You're not alive till you're doing it live,' as Gerry liked to say, in a way which – because it was Gerry saying it – somehow did not sound ridiculous.

She slowly lost touch with him after that for a long time, and could only watch from afar as he went on to bigger and better things – indeed, she looked forward to the day she could point to the latest BAFTA nominations and say, 'I took acid in a cemetery in Dalston with that bloke once!' But then, somewhere in the noughties, Gerry's star went *phut*. A new generation of writers and actors were elbowing their way to the fore and, after a couple of divorces and a spell in rehab, Gerry drifted – like Colleen – into safer, more lucrative options. These days he ran creative retreats on cruise ships and Greek islands for well-oiled, middle-aged divorcées looking to put their sadness behind them and spend their settlement money on discovering their inner selves. It was all a bit New Agey, he explained, but only in a chintzy, *Daily Mail*-ish sort of way.

Thanks to Gerry, Colleen had found herself four years ago spending a fortnight in a luxurious residential centre on the southern side of Crete, running daily sessions on Finding

Your Heart's Voice, Fearless Creativity, and Directing the Inner Drama of You. It was amazing what you could get away with if you looked and acted the part. 'Just make sure you have a sudden wild intuition every fifteen minutes or so,' Gerry had counselled. 'Be ditzy and unpredictable. Tell people they are complex and surprising. And if you ever get stuck, just clap your hands, put on a funny camp accent and shout: "*Energy*, people, *energy!*"'

Colleen studied her part well, and by the end of a week had become a minor local celebrity, adored and revered by her very own First Wives' Club. But what she'd really loved were the late-night chats with Gerry, moonwalking together over mountainous sand dunes and getting tiddly with a bottle of the local raki in their little cove's one taverna. Gerry was balding and arthritic now, a touch sadder and quieter than of old. But, being Gerry, he had the courage to be vulnerable, and her heart went out to him. Almost to her surprise, she found she still wanted him.

'So, how about it?' Gerry was saying now. 'Just you and me, and the Indian Ocean. Well, and the rest of the Higher Self team, obviously. Coral beaches, perfect seas, fragrant fifty-something devotees and all the fish curry and egg hoppers you can eat. Get the old dream team back together.' Gerry was launching his own holistic self-discovery centre on a private island off Sri Lanka, and he wanted Colleen to join the staff as Head of Creative Discovery. In practice, this meant teaching whatever she wanted, hiring whoever she wanted to assist her, and working for just six months a year. According to Gerry's calculations, they could charge enough for her to take the rest of the year off so she could spend some quality time writing again. He was buying a house out in Thailand, he said, and there'd be time and space for her to live and work there for some of the year too.

'I'm not exactly clear what you're offering me, Gerry.'

'I'm offering you as much as you want,' he said. 'I'm saying you can take what you need, or who you need, and make of it what you want.'

'The world on a stick.'

'If that's what you want, sure,' said Gerry, with maddening, intoxicating Gerry-ness.

'But you and me—' she tried.

'Shh,' he said soothingly. 'Nothing has to have a label.'

She laughed, tingling in spite of herself. 'That is *such* a Gerry thing to say.'

'Think about it.'

Just then, she heard a persistent tapping noise and looked up. Andrew was at the window. He was holding up a product and looking at her expectantly, with a delighted face that said, 'I've found the ones you like!'

She thought of Gerry's intelligent blue eyes and his long brown legs striding across a Cretan beach, and then she took in her service-station husband. He had the air of a minor civil servant, dressed as always in smart-casual M&S-type things and sensible squelchy shoes, even though he generally worked from home and could have done all his stuff in a sequinned mankini and pith helmet without anyone being the wiser; even though today he was supposed to be off on holiday with his wife, cutting free and starting over and rekindling the magic.

All his clothes were beige somehow, even the ones that weren't.

Andrew was taller than you realised, about 5' 11", but he wasn't exactly a physically imposing specimen. His arms had a weedy, slightly shrivelled quality, his little eyes hid behind glasses that were very George Smiley, and the rest of his bod sort of trailed off into nothing-at-all-ness. But this was the thing about Andrew, always had been; he was easy to over-look, almost invisible, but then he could say something funny or silly or insanely thoughtful, and suddenly his whole being came into delightful view. It was magic of a sort she rarely saw from him these days. But, as she remembered now, watching him mime a little dance to explain why she needed the product in question and how best to use it, and quite oblivious to the small crowd of onlookers he was attracting, he could be very silly indeed.

'Got to go,' Colleen said to her phone. She couldn't help giggling as she stuck up a thumb at Andrew to approve the purchase of three packs of Imodium Plus.

VII. THE ALPHA MALE OF SYNTAX

Andrew was at the wheel, and the mechanics of driving were slowly coming back to him. The miles ticked by, and there was even a decent conversation or two with Colleen. This often happened when he drove, as he had a good excuse for not looking at her.

When they tried to converse at other times Colleen almost inevitably became frustrated by his inability to make eye contact, which to her seemed a kind of blatant dishonesty. Colleen's gaze was strong and level and frank; it terrified the hell out of Andrew, a man who tended to say the opposite of what he meant, or not say it at all – especially if it really needed saying.

'I'm a communications expert!' she'd assert, whether on the sofa or round a pub table. 'Not making eye contact is just such a snub to the other person!' Or: 'I'm just so sick of look-ing at the side of your glasses.' Sometimes she would go through a whole evening pointedly *not looking* at him and refusing to make eye contact with him when she spoke, just to show him what it was like. Andrew knew he was being taught a lesson at such moments, but if he was honest he found a night off from the full beam of Colleen's gaze rather restful.

The car was littered with the detritus of food on the go: sandwich cartons, satsuma peel, coffee cups. The roads got narrower and busier. Stonehenge came and went, looming in the distance like an artfully shambolic pile of left luggage. The satnav went on with its remorseless wayfinding, the female voice sounding as ever like someone in the wrong job, someone on the verge of losing their patience with the incompetence of everyone around them.

Sheep stared blankly at Andrew from their fields. But that was OK, he didn't mind sheep. Horses were sinister, of course. Pigs were berks, donkeys were wankers. If the standard grammatical sentence was rendered as a farmyard, he mused suddenly, where syntactically would each animal fit?

The bull would have to be the verb of course, the alpha male of syntax. This would make the cows the nouns, which, though on one level a rather simplistic old-fashioned formulation, like male and female plug connectors, did sort of work. Cows were stubbornly static, thingy things after all, and so were nouns. The sheep were natural adjectives, milling about and quietly modifying whatever came their way. The horses could be the adverbs, that most suspect and problematic word class. The chickens could be the definite and indefinite articles, flapping about under everyone's feet; the donkeys, slow-moving but structurally influential, made for natural conjunctions. And the cats – always moving as they were over, up, under, through and around things – were the natural choice for the prepositions.

Mentally he stood back for a moment and surveyed his handiwork. Where did this all get him? God alone knew. But another few minutes had passed, and that surely was the game.

As the A roads gave way to the B roads, there were niggly exchanges about the right route, and the atmosphere in the car grew tense. Eventually Andrew drove past a tiny turn-off that looked like a driveway but which, half an hour later, would finally reveal itself as the top of the road that led to their actual destination. Colleen reminded him, perhaps more than once, that she had said to turn down this road in the first place. He retorted that it was thanks to her that they had done three laps of Truro and driven halfway to St Ives for no good reason.

'We're a team, darling,' said Colleen with heavy irony. 'My mistakes are your mistakes.'

It would be dark and raining when they finally arrived at their cottage. A dog barked, and a light came on in the big house next door. For a moment a silhouette in curlers appeared at a high window, then all was darkness again.

SUNDAY

Grandad's funny. We tell him what to do. He knows lots of games.

Granny's nice but she tells us off more. She's not very good at playing.

She always looks sad. Mum says it's coz she's got so much on her plate. But she doesn't eat much.

Grandad's so funny. We're going to get him with water and acorns and everything!

I. SO MUCH TRYING

Colleen sat in the bath, staring into space. She was lounging on a beach at the edge of time, a mere bubble of consciousness at play. She was someone and no one and everyone, deliriously engulfed in the foamy embrace of her soothing amniotic bathwater. A paperback lay open on the floor, spine splayed and wet pages half-folded, callous victim of her oceanic vibe . . .

What was this stuff called again? She reached lazily for the bottle. *Relaxing Bath Elixir.* Ooh, what a treat. She lay back on the thoughtfully placed inflatable bath pillow, and reviewed their time in the cottage so far.

Last night they had both been really trying. There had been so much trying. So . . . trying.

It had been getting dark by the time they arrived. The road was narrow and overhung with trees on one side while on the other, mysterious properties with deep driveways slunk back from inspection. Down and down they drove, slowly and carefully, Colleen squinting hard through her window for a sign to Red Barn Cottage.

'Oh, for a little light pollution right now,' said Andrew, in his best comedy snarky voice.

The lulled, cocooned feeling from all that enclosed car time – all that *in-car-ceration,* as Andrew would no doubt insist on calling it, she was getting as bad as him now – was rudely interrupted by an alarming scraping noise coming from the car's underside. Then, all the activity of arrival: car doors slamming, boot creaking open; panicked search on mobile for entry details. Phone-lit hunt for 'key under stone frog'. Locks, doors, alarm; in and out again and again with the bags, more doors and boot slamming (and no sodding drink at the end of it).

The moment of arrival at what both would call their 'holiday home', in deference to family breaks of yore, took her back to many similar moments with the children. How she had loved watching Ned and Sonja race around their new world, peering in cupboards, jumping on beds, opening doors, laughing at the toys and books and odd crannies they found, shouting out each new discovery. Every new holiday was a new beginning. They were hoping that Sonja might be able to pop over with the twins later this week, and Colleen smiled at the thought of her grandchildren running round and exploring the rooms the same way.

That first night, Andrew made a Thai red curry stir-fry thing while she nosed about. Their temporary home was a generous conversion, effectively three barns joined together in such a way as to form a squarish U-shape. One leg of the U contained a dining area and a long, sunken living room; the other leg contained two large en-suite bedrooms, each kitted out with ceramic bowls of lavender and patchouli potpourri, tasteful floral cushions and Laura Ashley bedding. The connecting arm contained a long, well-equipped kitchen and a bathroom complete with a proper Victorian bath with proper Victorian feet, the room tiled in various marine blues and ornamented with a tasteful selection of nautical knick-knacks. There seemed to be a lot of pine everywhere, and a lot of air freshener, and a lot of cushions; also, a lot of books about murder.

The book Colleen was now sort of reading was called *My Mother the Psychopath*. The various bookshelves around the cottage had a strong true-crime theme, she noticed. *Slave Girl – Return to Hell*. *Warrior Kings: The South London Gang Wars 1976–1982*, by Noel 'Razor' Smith. *Pure Evil: Inside the Minds and Crimes of Britain's Worst Criminals*. *The Cambridge Rapist – Unmasking the Beast of Bedsitland. Conversations with a Serial Killer*. And for light relief, *Who Killed Who?: The True Crime Bumper Quiz Book*.

The cottage, like every holiday home before it, offered Colleen a double-edged vision of envy and hope. She envied the situation of the world it evoked, the orderly contentment that must surely be enjoyed by any couple who were organised enough, not just to have a dust-buster and scented sanitising hand gel in every room, but to ensure that in every case their colours matched the room decor. She couldn't help imagining every immaculate room and picturesque village they came across on holiday as the blueprint of another life that they (she?) might have lived had they (she?) made better choices, lived a better or different way somehow. But there was hope here too, sometimes, because the orderliness and optimism of these thoughtful leisure-scapes gave her something to aspire to. During holiday weeks, therefore, her mind swung back and forth between 'Why can't my life be like this?' and 'Maybe we could run a little B & B here?'

Tired from the drive, they had eaten, not drunk, or only fizzy water, and spent a few minutes worrying over the cryptic crossword. The Saturday one was the hardest. Their aim would be to get the thing done by the end of the week, but that night – as was their ritual of old – the goal was just to solve one clue. Break the seal, get off the mark.

Eventually Andrew announced that he had 17 across: *Wedding transport held up? (6, 5)*. By long-held agreement, Colleen was now given a decent moment to look at the clue and work it out for herself before Andrew revealed his answer and, most importantly (to him at least) his explanation. Every element of a cryptic clue had to be accounted for, he stipulated, after which he would pronounce the clue either 'elegant' or something less flattering to the setter like 'awkward' or 'creaky'.

The official reason for this practice was to enable the other person to share in the fun of solving the clue: it was amazing how often, when one of them announced they had got one, the other would suddenly be able to solve it too. But the real – unspoken – reason was that it gave Colleen a chance to pre-empt another display of Andrew's preening pedantry. How clever he was! And how pleased he was to be so clever. *Clevercleverclever*, he went, like that don in Joyce mowing his lawn that, oh, so cleverly, he'd once told her about.

Clever. What a word. What an overrated virtue. 'There's nothing smart about being clever,' Colleen sometimes aphorised with clients who were guilty of over-thinking things. 'What does your gut say?' (Right now, her gut told her that the curry had perhaps been just a tiny bit too hot, but that the Imodium Plus had been an excellent purchase.)

That morning, Andrew had been up early, cutting up grapefruit and bringing her tea in bed. Colleen spent a pleasant half hour reading about *Britain's Top 10 Unexplained*

Murders. Soon they would both be at home a lot more, as she was supposed to be stepping back from client work now and focusing on the book that would allegedly help the business to sell. It was sort of about mindfulness, and sort of about self-esteem too. (Provisional title: *You Only Have Now!*). Andrew was at home most of the time already anyway, of course, except when he went off for the odd meeting with a client or agency.

Will it be like this every day now, she mused, a cuppa in bed and toast slotted neatly into, good Lord, a proper old swirly metal toast rack? Streaky bacon, real butter and a proper hen-shaped tea cosy? Would it buggery.

Still, he had been trying, bless him. He really had. *They* had been trying, bless *them.* In fact, if he'd hovered over her this morning instead of rushing off to boil the kettle, she might even have been tempted. Languorously, Colleen swished the still-warm bathwater between her legs, and thought of Gerry.

In the end, after dinner, they agreed to leave the clue unwritten, to allow Colleen a bit more thinking time when she was less tired. They adjourned to the TV area, where Colleen found a DVD of *Gladiator*, and they put this on almost at once because they both sort of liked it and they were trying, and because they knew from bitter experience that a proper discussion about what each of them really wanted to watch, who was more prepared to compromise, and who got their way with the remote most often, could so easily go off the rails.

I will . . . win the crowd, said Russell to Ollie, a line that Andrew had tried many times to imitate but somehow never could, not even to his usual level of a good-bad impression. But the film sucked them in, as it always did, and by the time Maximus reaches his burned-down home in Spain to discover that he is too late to save his wife and children, the tears were pouring freely beneath the frames of Andrew's glasses and down his smooth, pink cheeks.

She liked it in a way, when Andrew wept. The tears flowed free and true, and there was nothing clever about them.

II. SHADES OF BLACK

Andrew left Colleen in the bath and went back to his bed in the spare bedroom, where he'd spent most of the night exchanging clandestine messages with his son Ned.

He was cross with Ned for messaging him via his normal email, the one that *other people* (i.e. Colleen) could see when it popped up on the phone. They had their own platform they could use but, as Ned argued tersely in subsequent messages, Andrew hadn't picked up his last messages because he obviously hadn't logged in recently. And anyway, it wasn't easy to think straight, where his son was at.

Where Ned was *at* wasn't easy to work out, except that it was obviously somewhere like all the other places he'd been at for the last ten years or so. Someone wanted him burned because he hadn't paid for a score. He didn't feel well, he said, which was a classic Ned understatement that could mean any of a wide range of alarming symptoms.

The messages went back and forth irregularly for much of the night. Sometimes Ned's came one after another in a manic flurry. He sounded desperate, but that was standard too. It was a matter of trying to parse the current level of despair, to distinguish its particular shade of black from all the other shades of black he lived under. Andrew tried to talk to Ned about other things. Common interests from their past – the football, his sister, politics. He just wanted a sign that his son was still in there. But trying to engage Ned in a chat about Arsenal or his family or post-Brexit politics was a bit like trying to talk to a seal about global warming.

Basically, Ned only wanted to talk about one thing. He had one question to ask.

can you get me some cash dad

There was no point Andrew saying, *What about the electronic wallet thing that I top up for you and you empty month in, month out?* What they both knew Ned meant was, *Can you get me some more cash, Dad?*

you got to help dad

leg is bad.

got to pay or get away but can't

it was safer on the inside

Long before *other people* were stirring, Andrew made the treasonous transfer. In exchange, he had extracted a couple of half-promises about seeking help that weren't worth the Rizla paper they weren't written on. Colleen slept on next door, insulated from his treachery by earplugs and mouth-guard. If she woke and found him absent, he could always say that she'd been snoring, or tell her that *he* had been snoring and had woken her, she wouldn't remember. They slept in separate beds more than half the time at home now anyway, and snoring gave them both an easy pretext for the practice. Andrew liked to imagine they were like one of those gilded couples in an Evelyn Waugh novel, who each have their own separate state rooms as a matter of taste and prestige, only of course the couples in Waugh were no example to anyone.

When people found out that he and Colleen had separate bedrooms, he always blustered that snoring had ruined many a decent marriage, and that this was just a practical arrange-ment made in the interests of their relationship. They were hardly alone in this, were they? Hadn't there been that whole thing about it on *Woman's Hour?*

Only: once you started sleeping separately, the opportun-ities for sleeping not-separately did not come along so easily. Before, they could always have one of their rows, but at least fall exhausted into the same bed. However bad things got, they still came back together at night, even if only to snore loudly with bodies pointed away from one another. And then they would wake together the next morning, which felt at least like a first step in the latest truth and reconciliation process.

But now it was all too easy for Colleen to stomp off to her [their] room, and pull up the drawbridge behind her. The room was then sealed with the forcefield of her anger and outrage, and he didn't know how to even try to scale it. Sometimes he didn't want to, of course. Instead, he would sit scrolling through his phone on the sofa, draining off a glass or two, then make the slow walk up the stairs and across the landing, to settle wearily into the little den he was accumulating in his son's old room.

He could perhaps have tried setting up in Sonja's former bedroom, a far more tasteful and fragrant option even now, but that was their primary guest room and Colleen would almost certainly have vetoed the idea. Anyway, he liked Ned's room, with its old music posters [Foo Fighters, Red Hot Chili Peppers, The Cure], Ned's collection of Terry Pratchetts [someone Andrew couldn't get into at the time, though he read them now with *faux*-nostalgic pleasure], a battered skateboard and some old gaming consoles.

All Ned's other stuff had gone – anything that could be sold, basically – by the day he 'moved out'. But it still felt a bit like Ned in there. It still looked and smelt of *boy*.

It was the only uncomplicated place where he could just lie down and miss his son.

After sleeping fitfully till about 5am, Andrew checked his messages and slipped along the corridor into the bedroom, so he could wake up next to Colleen. As he was stealthily shedding his dressing gown, Andrew's eye was drawn to a light that had come on in the big house.

31

A man sat at the window, face side on. He looked like he was concentrating on some unseen task. Andrew loved looking into windows, loved peering into passing lives from a train carriage. Often, at night, he would stare into the row of houses that backed onto his home: a whole dashboard of private half-glimpsed scenes to savour, a prospect that felt part Ayckbourn and part Hitchcock.

For a moment the man looked across at Andrew in the dark. He had white tufts of hair either side of a big expanse of baldness. It was the face of an older man, but it had a surprising sort of forcefulness about it. The lower half of the face was dominated by a pair of deep creases that gave it a sort of permanent dramatic downward smile. It made Andrew think of Mr Punch, or one of those creepy horror-film clowns.

The man looked over at Andrew and Colleen's room, seeming for a moment to look right through the darkness to meet Andrew's eye. A dog barked. Andrew couldn't be seen, of course, so it was curious when the man's whole face cracked into an even wider grin, and he appeared to give a little wave.

III. WISH YOU WERE HERE?

'Guess what?'

'What?'

'The beach is about ten shitting miles away.'

Colleen, emerging from her lie-in sharp and purposeful, had decided that a drive round the local area was in order. Find the beach, work out where the shops are, find the nearest town, get the paper, stock up on a few essentials and non-essentials (she fancied steak tonight, also they needed wholegrain mustard) (also she fancied rosé; wine boxes were so practical).

'O knight,' said Andrew, reading her mind. 'Thou lackest a cup of canary.'

'What are you talking about?' she snapped. She was quietly furious to discover that their holiday home, according to one of the many maps provided of the local area, was in the middle of a forest.

They actually knew next to nothing about their destination. On the website, the cottage pics had included several views of a sweeping expanse of lovely sandy-looking beach, on the basis of which they had easily been able to groupthink the firm idea that the cottage was a few hundred yards at most from the sea. Before he put through the booking – and before the arrival of the email from their mutual friends, the two Pauls – Andrew conjured up for her evening strolls to the beach, window seats with the crossword in a little fish restaurant, *aperitifs* and *digestifs*, cute little pats of butter and *I think I'll start with the soup*, a bottle of something cold and crisp, *what do you recommend?*, walking home arm in arm to an elemental soundtrack of distant waves breaking in the dark salt air.

In reality, the nearest shop was about three miles down the road, an old-fashioned village store with a petrol pump squatting in front of it, its defunct hose still tucked on a sarcastic hip. Andrew and Colleen found the place after driving around for a good half an hour along narrow, winding lanes that left their satnav suddenly tentative and confused.

Inside, the shop smelled of long-heated greasy pies and mothballs. Filled rolls were made to order, according to a chipped, half-hidden sign at the counter that dared you to ask for one; cashback was allegedly also available. Another sign said cheerily: 'Sorry: we don't accept credit – or euros!' In one corner there was a limited selection of unconvincing beach items: a small range of tiny buckets and spades that looked as if they'd snap the moment they came into contact with wet sand; a couple of shrimp nets stapled flimsily to their wooden frames; a stand of dusty sandcastle flags and spinning windmills whose sails had been left to unfurl.

'You here for the week then?' the woman behind the counter asked, sizing them up.

'That's right. Till Saturday.'

'Staying anywhere nice?'

'Up at Red Barn Cottage. Do you know it?'

The woman paused with her till tray open, inspecting their change for a surprisingly long time.

'He still at it then, is he?' she said at last.

Andrew thought suddenly of the clown at the window. 'The owners, do you mean? We haven't really met them properly.'

Colleen looked at him oddly. 'We haven't met them *at all*, have we?'

The woman nodded, mostly to herself. She slammed the till drawer shut with her hip, and handed over their change.

'Anyway, looks like you've brought the fine weather with you,' she said at last.

Outside the shop, they began their first row of the week.

Colleen felt that they were the butt of some obscure local joke. She felt scratchy and sober. Her stomach had started again, and she could feel a headache coming on.

'I cannot believe you've suckered us into this place.' Earlier that morning, Gerry had sent a message that simply said, *#wishyouwerehere?* The accompanying pic was a Sri Lankan beach bar. Gerry sat on a stool, mugging broadly with the barman, miming an attack on some brightly coloured drink with several umbrellas in it. Behind the pair of them, she glimpsed – as no doubt she was meant to – an endless expanse of gently shelving coral sand and serene, crystal-blue sea.

'What's wrong with it?'

'It's in the middle of sodding nowhere. The sea is miles away. Did you just stick a needle in the internet?'

'At least I booked something. If we'd left it to you, we'd still be in London.'

Still in London. It had a nice ring to it.

They walked past a building with seats and benches outside and a familiar sort of high, swinging sign. The Rose and Crown, it was called. She looked at it wistfully, while at the same time taking care to disguise her wistfulness. She looked at Andrew. There was a furtive expression on his face, as if he were engaged in a similar battle for self-mastery. She hated him for this, and looked around for another missile.

'*And* you've buggered the car.' It was making an odd clicking sound when they drove now.

To be fair, she had not had much involvement in the holiday booking. Also, to be totally fair, the car scraping its underside on the driveway would probably have happened anyway, whoever had been driving. It would be easy to avoid the really steep bit in the day but, in the dark, turning in there for the first time, it was just a bit of a lottery.

But this was not a time to be fair.

'It's just typical of you. Slapdash short cuts. Always take the easy way out.'

'How is spending a whole day in a car with you any sort of an easy way out?'

'You knew I wanted to go to Greece or Spain. Italy. Malta.'

Andrew snorted. '*Malta?* When have you even uttered the word *Malta* before?'

It was possible that he didn't know some of these destinations were on her wish-list, she would reflect later, as she had only just thought of them herself.

'What are you talking about?' Andrew was saying now. 'I ran this place by you and you were really happy. *You* said it would be nice not to have to fly. *You* said you loved the idea of just driving for a few hours and already being on holiday the moment you arrived.'

'Oh, for God's sake. I only said that to be nice. You'd taken so long to organise even this, I couldn't face watching you going through it all over again and getting it even more wrong.'

They were still in the street, each with a hand on a door, snapping at each other across the car roof. A mum with a buggy and a toddler on a scooter quickly shepherded her children away from them.

Andrew looked stung. 'So much for our week of getting back on track,' he said quietly.

Another message. Colleen looked at her phone, and squealed with delight, the row apparently forgotten.

'It's Sonja!' she said, meeting his eyes for the first time since they'd left the house. 'They're coming tomorrow! About three.'

'Brilliant,' said Andrew. 'We'll just have to keep our brave faces on till after they've gone.'

'Oh, shut up,' she said, dismissing the last fifteen minutes with a sweep of her hand. 'That was just a bit of banter.' It was really, by their standards.

'Yes, m'lady,' said Andrew with heavy sarcasm, but she saw out of the corner of her eye that he couldn't help a small smile escaping. She'd been a little unfair, perhaps, and they both knew it, but he hadn't pressed home his advantage. The twins were coming, after all, and they were obsessed with their crazy silly grandad. He was probably even more excited than she was.

The twins were coming. It was something they could agree to be happy about.

IV. WELCOME PACK

Back at the cottage, Andrew and Colleen discovered a big bundle of goodies on display on their kitchen table. There was a bottle of the local apple juice (non-alcoholic). A home-made sponge cake dusted with icing sugar and wrapped neatly in cling film. Six eggs in a rough cardboard carton, eggs that looked fresher and bigger and tastier than the ones they got back home (as townies like her doubtless always said). And a pot of home-made blueberry jam, complete with a little doily lid sealed with an elastic band, just as her own mother used to do.

This charming bundle was accompanied by a bulging folder of leaflets about the local area – something they'd looked for in vain the previous night. It contained Indian takeaway menus, minicab cards, brochures for steam railways and craft museums, printouts of current film and theatre listings, even details of various holistic therapists and a local provider of spare parts for mobility scooters. There was everything you could wish for, and most of it no more than a tortuous half-hour drive away.

On the table, there was also a small envelope with a card in. The picture on the card was a floral bouquet of a rather generic sort, and inside there was a handwritten message in an ornate elegant hand that made Colleen think instinctively of her grandmother:

Welcome to Red Barn Cottage! We hope you have a lovely stay. Anything you need, we're watching out for you. Just knock on the big red door!

Underneath this charming message was a big mess of a signature that was quite impossible to decipher, other than that it began with an ostentatious cursive W.

The final element was a bottle of red wine. Not an especially classy vintage, Colleen noticed, cursing her own snobbery, but definitely a full one. Tenderly inspecting the elements of the welcome pack one after another, Colleen was touched by the generosity of the gesture. It was incredible really, the difference a little personal touch could make. Potpourri can only get you so far.

She felt Andrew behind her. He was nuzzling her neck, a habit she tended to hate but was actually quite receptive to now.

'Sorry about before,' he whispered.

She arched an arm round behind her and tousled the back of his head, careful not to convey any special consciousness of his bald patch, something she knew he was sensitive about. The male pattern thing was cruel on, well, males.

'It wasn't you, it was me,' she whispered. He was leaning into the back of her, he was inhaling her. She could feel him, and she could feel herself responding.

She had just turned back to him, lips half-parted ready for his, when there was a loud, unignorable rapping at the back door, accompanied by some excitable yapping.

'Hello hello hello! There is a Wolf at the door!'

V. DODGY SIGNAL

'Call me Wolf,' the man said again, as he stared into the bottom of his coffee cup, gently swilling the last inch of liquid. His accent had a trace of German but something else too – West Country perhaps. Wolf must be short for Wolf-gang, Andrew said later.

'Shut up, Jack!' Wolf shouted through the window. His dog, some sort of miniature German shepherd cross, stayed at the cottage threshold, no doubt trained not to enter in the presence of guests. He'd been sitting quietly at his post, but hearing Wolf talk, he couldn't resist a few barks. But when Wolf barked back, Jack gave a small submissive whimper and fell silent.

Wolf's face, glimpsed once by her husband in the distant dark, came into vivid focus up close. He had very blue twinkling eyes, a strong angular nose and a deep perma-grin that had something willed about it: Colleen had the impression of a man who *made* himself laugh a lot.

He was tall and spry, with a slight stoop and a dramatic tuft of white hair above each ear. His pale, pinkish skin was surprisingly wrinkle-free, except for little clusters of laughter lines. There was an energy about him that belied his years. Whenever Andrew asked him a practical question, about the boiler or the Wi-Fi or the recycling bin, he would leap to his feet and bound about the cottage, answering questions on the move, extracting manuals from drawers and pointing out notices on the wall. Nothing was too much trouble. Colleen was touched over and over by his excessive helpfulness.

'Thank you *so* much for our welcome pack,' she said. 'You really shouldn't have gone to all that trouble.' Then, keen to undercut her own cliché and underline her sincerity, she added, 'Though I'm very glad you did.'

'No, no. No,' he said, shaking his head, as if to deny all knowledge of the goodies. 'Mrs Wolf would never forgive me if we didn't welcome our guests properly. And she is right of course.'

'The cake and jam – did she make . . . Did you?'

'Oh, that's all her handiwork,' he said proudly. 'I helped out a little, but only under her strict direction.'

'Well, you must thank her,' said Colleen.

'From us,' Andrew put in.

'It's really very kind,' Colleen said now. 'Of both of you.' God, thanking people was hard. Finding the right words, knowing when to stop. The only thing that seemed to be harder than thanking people was *being thanked*, she thought, looking at Wolf shaking his head yet again.

'Stop!' he said, raising both palms with comic emphasis. 'It is our pleasure.'

They stopped.

'OK! Now I get out of your hair,' he said suddenly, shaking hands with them both again. 'Now if there's anything you need . . . anything at all, just knock on the door of the big house. Come on, Jack!'

Colleen followed his gaze through the window and looked out at Wolf's place. It was a sprawling Victorian pile, with at least three floors, surrounded by flower beds and rockeries and pretty climbing plants on all sides. Colleen made out hollyhocks and wisteria and roses; towards the rear, a cluster of birds buzzed and tweeted around a prettily complex jumble of hanging feeders and bird tables. The brick was that lovely deep red you never seem to get in newer houses, and a plume of smoke billowed merrily from one of the gabled chimney stacks on the roof.

It was, thought Colleen, the sort of place where everyone's beloved grandparents should live. It was the sort of delight-fully baggy house that a child could lose themselves in for hours, the sort of place a classic family feel-good movie might be set. Years later, when adult life had messed you up good and proper and you were looking for some sort of healing or closure, and you found yourself doing some sort of visualis-ation exercise in a meditation class or hypnotherapy session, and they said to you, *Think of a place where you always felt happy and safe . . . this* would be the sort of place. Your mind would recall in loving detail the home-made swing hanging lopsided on the willow; the secret passage between the lawn and the veg patch; the pattern in the apple-tree bark that looked like a face. OK, this was her own gran's home she was thinking of now; but still.

'Now, vere vere we?'

Wolf had gone whistling out the door, striding back towards his house with the air of a man happy in his work, and Andrew was back nuzzling and grinding again, only now with a cod Nazi accent. The cogs of their lust clicked neatly into place, or at least they would have had Colleen's phone not gone off.

'It's Sonja!' cried Colleen.

'Leave it,' said Andrew, in what she knew was his best seductive voice. 'She'll call back.'

'I better take it. The signal is so dodgy round here.' Andrew emitted a low sound.

'Hello, darling!' Colleen went striding off out of the kitchen and into the courtyard, where she began pacing crunchy zigzag patterns in the gravel, in search of the one elusive spot that would give her a second bar on her phone.

Sonja had little to say beyond the message Colleen had already seen, but it was lovely to hear her voice, and hear the twins shouting and giggling in the background.

'We'll be there about two tomorrow, OK?'

'Why don't you come a bit earlier and we can have lunch? What time do the little ones eat?'

'Best not, Mum, thanks. They'll be starving by 12.30. We'll grab something on the way. It's quite a long drive from Wales.'

'OK, love. You take care on the roads.'

'Will do. And, Mum?'

'Yes, love?'

'Try not to get in too much candy and chocolate and stuff? I'm worried they're looking a bit . . . chubby. Billy especially.'

'Jesus! They're only four.'

'That's when it starts, Mum! And if they put it on now, it's hard to undo later. The fat cells!'

'All right, all right. We'll get the cucumber and carrot sticks ready.'

There was a pause. In the background, Colleen heard the unmistakable theme tune of *Peppa Pig*.

'Mum?' said her daughter. 'Have you heard anything?'

Colleen stiffened. 'Anything what?' she said. It came out fiercer than she meant.

Another pause. 'Oh, nothing. We'll see you tomorrow. Bye for now!'

'Looking forward to it! Bye, love.'

As she tucked her phone in her pocket, she became aware of a plaintive mewling. For some reason, her first thought was of a baby in a basket, abandoned at the door of a cottage hospital. She took a few steps round to the side of their place, to where the bins were. A tiny black cat, with a white face and a white triangle on its chest, was balanced neatly on the top of a fence. She made her best cat-befriending noise, a sort of gentle sucking/squelching sound that she had perfected over many years of chance feline interactions, and stretched out an unthreatening pair of fingers. The little cat managed to look both terrified and intrigued at once. But then a loud burst of barking broke into the morning quiet (Jack, in the distance, probably), and when Colleen looked back to the fence, the cat had vanished.

Back in the house, she found that Andrew had settled on the bed with a cup of tea and a copy of *Belgian Serial Killers: An Overview*. The moment had been and gone; indeed, she had almost forgotten there had ever been a moment. But Andrew was clearly hoping against hope that they might pick things up again. He wouldn't say anything, of course; but, you know, there he was half in bed in the middle of the day, just in case, you know.

Sonja would have phoned back, of course she would have. Colleen could have ignored the call, could have gone with the flow, as she'd had every intention of doing, as for a good moment she'd really wanted to, as much perhaps as Andrew. But when the phone rang she had a sudden out-of-body glimpse of herself, of them both, as if from far above. She saw two people clinging together on a precipice without foundation, two people pretending they were still

OK. She shivered at what she saw, and she suddenly had to get away.

Colleen busied herself in the en-suite with her second shower of the day, to go with the one she'd had after her bath.

'What shall we do tonight?' Andrew called out to her from the bed.

'I don't know, love,' she said. 'Maybe dinner somewhere and the crossword?' Dinner would be a sodding drive away, of course. She thought of their historic tussles about designated drivers.

'Or we could order in?' he called. 'What do you fancy?'

'I want a fucking drink!' she screamed to herself over the sudden roar of the shower. A scream doesn't have to be that loud to be a scream.

'What's that, love?' he called. From outside she heard a few barks – Jack, no doubt.

'Oh, anything,' she shouted back. 'Not Chinese.' She didn't know why he bothered asking, they'd been ordering takeaways the same way for years. She'd veto Chinese, he'd veto Thai, and then what else was there really if not Indian, and she always wanted the side thing with spinach in, and he always insisted on garlic naan instead of paratha, and she always suggested something with prawns in, and he'd be tempted by something vegetarian, a daal perhaps, but she'd be less than keen. And then they'd always, always, *always* end up with lamb rogan josh and chicken murgh masala.

Their local friendly Indian (technically a Bangladeshi, as Andrew liked to remind her *every single time*) always delivered half a dozen of the big cold Cobras if you slipped them an extra fiver.

The twins are coming tomorrow, she said to herself, biting experimentally into the fleshy part of an upper arm. *Hold that thought.*

43

VI. INTO THE WOODS

After a late lunch of omelette and salad – made with Wolf's farm-fresh eggs, and with each protesting loudly to the other that they *really could* taste the difference – Andrew and Colleen decided to venture into the woods.

Their cottage stood about fifty feet from the main house. Their car sat on a gravelled courtyard in the centre of its U-shaped plan, the open end of which was diagonally pointed at Mr and Mrs Wolf's big house. [Was Wolf a surname or a first name? How was his first name Wolf yet she was called Mrs Wolf? It wasn't clear. Or was the surname perhaps Woolf, as in Virginia?] Behind the cottage there was a thin but interesting garden of steep terraced rockeries and landscaped beds, which quickly rose up to the level of the kitchen windows; when washing something at the sink, you looked straight into a high sloping bank of succulents. The garden ran the length of the rear of the cottage and along behind one leg of the U to join up with one edge of the big house's garden. At its other end it was bounded by a hedge, beyond which ran the road. The hedge ran all the way around the perimeter of the cottage garden, in fact; when Andrew climbed up a bank to look over it, he saw only a series of ploughed fields surrounding a wooded area further off. Contrary to their ill-researched expectations, it was very definitely a landscape and not a seascape, whichever way you looked.

The road that ran alongside the cottage was a narrow, metalled track which allowed only for single-file traffic. Cars came down the road very rarely, but they absolutely flew past when they did. Round here, Andrew quickly realised, you always had to remember the last passing point you'd seen, as you never knew when you'd next need one. You could drive for miles and see nothing, then come round a sharp blind bend and find yourself in a sudden standoff with a postal van or a Calorgas lorry.

Over the road, in a bosky stretch between two wide drive-ways, there was a pathway that Wolf had told them about, a public right of way that led into woods.

'This is when you need a dog,' panted Colleen, as she clambered over the stile that marked the entrance to the wood.

'Bit life-affirming for us, isn't it, a dog?' countered Andrew, affecting great confidence as he swung a leg over. 'We're cat people, aren't we, surely?'

'People are allowed to change.'

This remark alarmed him because cats were an article of faith between them. They had never been without cats, and always at least two, so that they had company for each other. It was true that the current pair, Midge and Mogadoo – named aeons ago by their own twins – were approaching their end days now, and neither was much fun any more. Midge barely moved all day and emitted fearsome smells; Mogadoo spent a lot of time reversing into walls. But still, he knew that he would weep when each of them left, and would as always spend way too much time pondering the best way to mark their departure. They were family, and more depend-able and easier to love than some.

Neither spouse was very well dressed for woods, as it turned out. Andrew had canvas deck shoes on, and Colleen had plumped for something strappy. The woods were pretty enough, except that the terrain was unexpectedly hard-going. The sun obviously never penetrated the thick deciduous cover, and it was surprisingly muddy. But the mud had an unexpected sandy quality too, that sucked at their feet and made walking disagreeably hard work. It was a night-mare, basically. [A *quag-mare?*]

Andrew thought of telling Colleen his new word, but it wasn't one of his best. In any case, she was staring rapt at her phone, a secretive smile playing on her face.

'Is that the twins again?' he called.

She looked up abruptly. 'OK,' she said after a pause, a response which, he noted, acknowledged his question without actually answering it. 'They're coming at two. Tomorrow,'

'Yeah. We know.'

'Oh, yeah, right. Just confirming.'

He got out his phone and looked at their family WhatsApp group. 'Circle of Trust', it was called. [He'd originally wanted to call it 'Square of Care', since there were of course four in the immediate family, but Colleen had vetoed the name, as he should have guessed.]

'You're doing well,' he said. 'I can't get a signal in here.' She seemed to spend more and more time looking and smiling at her phone these days.

'Andrew,' she said.

'Yeeees,' he said, wondering frantically whether she wanted to have forest sex with him or divorce him, he really had no idea.

'Can I be honest with you?'

His heart thumped. 'Go on.'

'I know we've only just set out . . . but I'm finding this walk a bit shite,' she said, pointing to her spattered leggings and her mud-choked vintage summer beach sandals with the rhinestone detail on the toe straps. 'Can we go back and get some tea?'

It was yet another thing they could agree on. He smiled with relief and threw a big squishy arm around her.

'Only if you promise to put in some serious work on seventeen across.'

He flipped them around and back towards the stile, embarrassingly only about fifty yards away.

'Back to the future!' he shouted, with hope in his heart.

VII. AN EXPANSIVE TWINKLE

When they got back, Colleen sent a quick text to Gerry. *Don't hassle. Thinking x.* She wasn't sure it went through.

Andrew was obviously having problems too, because he was soon off to the big house to ask Wolf about the Wi-Fi. If they couldn't get it to work, it would not only mean that they couldn't send or receive messages, but also that they wouldn't be able to stream stuff.

She couldn't imagine how she and Andrew would get through the week without box sets and movies. They were so wonderfully time-consuming.

'If you're frying bacon, it's better to use the green frying pan,' Wolf was saying to Andrew as they came back in. 'With the small black one, the handle can easily catch on the gas flame, like you've done here. See?' He was at the draining board now, pointing to a little melted dent in the handle. 'Be quiet, Jack!' he shouted to his dog. The door was half-open, and Jack was keen as always to get inside with his master.

'Right, right,' said Andrew contritely. 'Sorry about that.'

'Oh, it's not you, it's everyone,' said Wolf generously. 'Just the usual wear and tear. But still, good to avoid things where we can.'

'Do you want to bring your dog in?' said Colleen. 'We really don't mind.'

'Oh, that's very kind of you,' said Wolf. 'But I don't want to give him ideas. And besides,' he said with a comically adversarial leer, 'he's not very good with . . . cat people.'

'How did you know we have cats?' asked Colleen, amazed. She thought of the little black cat. It had to be a stray; there was no way it was Wolf's.

'Well, I know you don't have a dog,' said Wolf. 'So I took a shot!'

After accepting Colleen's offer of a cup of coffee, Wolf went into the living room, where he began playing with routers and login codes and Andrew's smartphone. Something was not as he expected, judging by his quizzical noises and grimaces of good-natured exasperation.

While he was working away on their behalf, she and Andrew felt oddly powerless as to what to do or how to even *be* around him. It seemed rude to just get on with their own thing, as if he was a tradesperson they had summoned, who would later invoice them for their time; on the other hand, he was clearly running through a well-rehearsed trouble-shooting routine of his own, and had absolutely no need of their help. Colleen rearranged the coffee things for a third time, while Andrew scrubbed impotently at the frying pan handle.

Eventually, Wolf returned to the kitchen. 'Something is rotten in the state of . . . *Vodaphonia*,' he announced at last, taking a big swig of his coffee and exhaling with loud satisfaction.

Colleen snorted in Andrew's direction. 'That's exactly the sort of thing *you'd* say.' She laughed.

'I think I *have* said that, before now,' said Andrew wonderingly.

'But worry not, I have a solution found,' said Wolf. 'Or rather, I have found a solution.' Already, out of the corner of her eye, and oh dear God, she could see Andrew preparing some informal remarks about German sentence structure.

'What I've done is to put you on my home network, rather than the cottage's own one. That one seems to be working fine, so you can just piggyback onto us – and we can just share the signal together!' He seemed very pleased with this, and – if it meant Netflix was back – then so were they.

'That's brilliant, thanks ever so much,' said Andrew.

'Not at all, not all.' He laughed, shaking his head. 'All part of the service.'

There was a silence. As if in confirmation of his good work, Colleen's phone buzzed. It was Gerry: *I wish to keep only the 'you' of 'I love you'. The rest is yours.*

She coloured for a moment, then looked up quickly. 'Yes, thanks again. So *much*,' she said, hoping her brief absence from the conversation hadn't been noted.

'By the way, if you are going into the woods, there are some wellies in the cupboard in the porch that you are most welcome to take advantage of.'

'OK. Thanks.'

'Not at all! Could save you getting your beachwear muddy perhaps.'

Colleen smiled ruefully. 'Bit too late for that, I'm afraid.'

'Of course. But maybe next time.' He looked up at the deep tiled shelf over the kitchen sink, where his bottle of red remained unopened.

Oh, Gerry, she thought. *Always raising the stakes. Always upping the ante. Always wanting more.*

'I see you haven't attacked the wine yet?'

'No,' both Colleen and Andrew said, their oddly emphatic replies overlapping awkwardly.

'It's. Well. What it is, is . . .' Andrew couldn't find a way to finish his sentence, it seemed, which was a first.

'We're saving it up,' Colleen rescued him. 'For a special night.'

'But the eggs were lovely,' said Andrew. 'Farm fresh!'

'You really *can* taste the difference,' she put in.

'And we've attacked half of that sponge cake too.'

'Good, good!' Wolf beamed. 'Oh! By the way. If you have children coming, there are a few games and toys in a box in the wardrobe in the other bedroom.'

'Oh, that'll come in handy,' said Colleen, who'd already found them on her first recce of the cottage. A rather random selection of card books, matchbox cars and bits of

Lego. 'We've got the grandchildren coming tomorrow actually.'

'That's often the way.' Wolf smiled, with the seasoned wisdom of a village elder.

'Err – if that's OK?' Andrew put in nervously. 'You don't mind if they stay over a night?'

'Of course not, of course!' said Wolf with an expansive twinkle. 'The more the merrier! If the little ones pop round some time after lunch tomorrow, we may have a little something for them. Mrs Wolf would never forgive me if she were to miss them.'

'Oh, that's very sweet. I'm sure they'd love to.' She wanted to call him Wolf, but the name wouldn't come out. Was it because she still wasn't sure if it was a surname or a first name? Or was it both? Was he in fact called Wolf Wolf? Or was it because she worried his name was actually just 'Wolf', not even short for Wolfgang, and this was hard to process as a name for an elderly continental gentleman of a certain refinement, rather than, say, a New Age blacksmith living in an artisanal cooperative somewhere on the South Downs?

She couldn't help smiling to herself as she played with these thoughts. Andrew, she noticed, was eyeing her curiously.

'Well. Now I must go and sort out our dinner. Jack!'

'Very nice,' said Colleen. 'And what's it going to be?'

Wolf smiled thoughtfully, a hand on the back of a chair. His dog was barking and circling excitedly outside, desperate to know what the hold-up was. 'I am feeling a tad lazy,' he said at last. 'We might treat ourselves to an Indian takeaway.' He inspected the contents of the cafetière, saw no liquid left beyond the grounds, and stood up.

At the door he stopped. 'And of course, the children are welcome to play up on the meadow if they want to kick a ball or play tag or shoot some arrows or something.' The meadow, she guessed, must be the little field that stood beyond the big house and its garden. It was to the left of the house as you drove in, or on the right as you walked out, a raised flat area of thick wiry grass with a paddock gate, its full extent hidden by a tall hedge that ran down the far side of Wolf's house.

'Oh, they'd love that – keep them off the telly for a bit,' said Colleen, running effortlessly through the small gears of her small talk.

'Quite so,' said Wolf. 'Give them a chance to let off steam after their big drive.'

VIII. TOWARDS AND AWAY

'Shall I wear the yellow or the blue?' asked Colleen, holding up two similar dresses of a simple, strappy style.

'The yellow, definitely,' said Andrew, with a smile. 'It makes you look younger.' This was textbook, husband-101 stuff: always take questions about appearance and outfits very seriously, give them your full attention. Always give a positive answer. Never hesitate, never show fear. Never say something doesn't suit her. Never say she looks fat in anything. Her bum *does not look big, full stop*; not in that, not in anything. But while these are of course always the right answers, they must never sound pat; you have to take care to weigh each instance of the question, size up each individual outfit. But don't take too long about it either, or she'll sense doubt or deception in your answer. [Interesting word, *pat*.]

Such were the rules, to be obeyed with extreme prejudice, no matter how much she protested about wanting you to be really honest, to tell her straight, how she'd rather know what you *really* thought etc. We'd made that mistake before, goodness knows, learned the hard way.

They were on holiday. They needed to get out of the house, to do something holiday-ish. The dress was a good sign. A sign they were officially going out. The Indian could wait.

And anyway, he had no need to lie or even to euphemise, because he did like it, very much. He liked the way it set off her figure, the way it highlighted her bare neck and her strong shoulders. He liked it all. He loved her skin, her smell, her smile. He wanted to touch her. But he did not know if that was a good idea. He thought that it was probably best to wait for her to come to him. Only: what if she never did? What if she was thinking the same thing, unable to respond till he made the first move?

He thought of the first time they kissed. 'I sat on that sofa for bloody hours, dying of exposure,' she told him later. She'd been willing him to come over to her all night at that party, it transpired, while he'd been making trips to the kitchen, taking little nips of something random – vermouth? brandy? – to screw up the courage. He had been crap and cowardly, but still he forgave his younger self. The stakes had been so desperately high. *He had wanted her so much. Crossing over to that sofa was like walking a tightrope over the abyss. Nirvana potentially awaited him on the far side. But plummeting to his psychic death on the sharp rocks of despair far below seemed a much more likely outcome.*

The car creaked up the long narrow road, in the opposite direction to the village shop with the crap beach gear. This time they would find the actual sea, dammit.

Eventually, after only a handful of U-turns and a show-down with a tow truck, they were in a place called Saint something. A place that was actually next to the sea. They parked easily enough, in a half-empty public car park by a big public convenience. The beach lay ahead of them, an expanse of paler shadow in the dwindling light. The hill to the left, high and distant, was dotted with idiosyncratic holiday villas; to the right, the hill came right down to meet them, veined with sandy footpaths that the eye could follow as they meandered all the way up and doubtless over the headland.

In between these high points, they found a pretty seaside village with a few shops, a launderette and a couple of seafood places. The whole place was dominated by a large caravan park a little further up the road, which to Andrew's timorous middle-class eye loomed menacingly over the settlement like a parasitic cuckoo chick, an over-developed child set to devour its parent.

As if to confirm his fears, a gaggle of bored-looking topless gangly lads circled around aimlessly on bikes that would have been too small for them even without the saddles provocatively set to the lowest possible position. These youths seemed harmless enough, but of course you never can tell: all that strength and energy, without the slightest sense of responsibility. Teenagers terrified him.

They quickly found the eaterie they wanted, with its artfully distressed facade and chalk cursive signs promising a diverse selection of fresh fish daily. 'Our menu changes all the time – we cook what the fishers bring in!' said the sign proudly. Andrew noted with interest the use of the gender-neutral *fisher* and mentally filed it alongside *firefighter, postal worker, flight attendant* and of course the rebooted *actor*. Clearly this was their kind of restaurant, and they would have piled in and got stuck into the starters right there and then, were it not for the big CLOSED sign.

It was Sunday after all. They headed instead to the fish bar, Captain Haddock & Co, and ordered *takeaway cod and chips twice, please, with one gherkin and one mushy peas*. Takeaway was the obvious choice, since eating in meant perching on two of the three stools lined up beneath a giant shrimp-shaped mirror opposite the fryers, with nothing to look at but a wallchart of British sea-fish and a dodgy-looking bloke who kept licking his wet lips and pouring pound coins into a fruit machine. They walked with their food down to the beach, past the rather inviting and boisterous sounds emanating from the pub, and onto the sand, where Colleen cut her toe on a ring pull, and wished she'd never worn heels and a dress, and Andrew dropped his fish in the sand trying to catch her.

He went back to the fish bar and told them what had happened, secretly hoping they would take pity on him and give him some free fish. But they didn't, of course, so he cravenly forked out for another large cod and fetched a blanket from the car.

They sat there in the breezy half-dark, not exactly cold but not exactly warm or comfortable either, and it was almost easy to pretend that theirs was a companionable silence. At one point, Colleen leaned across Andrew and he dared hope for a split second that she wanted to kiss him. He reached out his hand, which landed fortuitously on a breast, only not that fortuitously perhaps, more *gratuitously* as it turned out, since Colleen was just stretching for an extra packet of pepper.

It had been eleven weeks and three days since he and Colleen had last made love – not that it mattered of course, not that it meant anything, not that he was counting. He squeezed the last remaining ketchup sachet on the blanket next to him. Under the pressure of his thumb and finger, it bulged ominously but it did not burst.

After chucking half their food away – because that was the thing about a fish-and-chip dinner, you suddenly remembered that you hadn't had one for ages and you really wanted one, but then you ate all that batter and starch and suddenly you had that horrible indigestible bread-neck feeling and you felt greasy all over and your clothes stank and then you felt like you never wanted fish and chips ever again – they walked along the shore, in a parody of romance. Colleen hadn't spoken for a good half an hour. It felt like the aftermath of a row, only without the row.

Andrew looked at the sea, and in the low dark waves he made out a polystyrene tray, of the sort they'd just been eating from. He noticed how the tray was swept in and then out again, in a perpetual motion of towards and away, but how underlying this pattern was a deeper, subtly remorseless outward trend that was slowly dragging the tray further from shore. And it struck him that this was very much like grief, for him at least. The memory of loss kept coming back, kept nudging your memory, but slowly, very slowly, underneath all that, the movement of mind and time was pushing the pain away, leaving only a drowned numb feeling in its wake. He was thinking of Ned, his son, who was not dead as such but was certainly lost to them. He would have liked to talk to Colleen about this, and how he or they might reverse the tide in some way, or just pool their feelings of sadness. And this would surely very much have been the moment, were it not that to do so would be to firebomb the fragile truce they had been constructing together over the last few days.

But still, he could not help feeling what he felt. And he could not help doing what he did.

'It looks nice in there,' he said, as they walked back together past the pub.

'*Come* on,' she said, almost gently, pulling him past. It was a tiny gesture, but one that filled him with great hope, more even than the fact that earlier that afternoon his wife had almost consented to kiss him.

As they drove back, the car's clicking turned into a more alarming grating, the sound of some fast-moving metal component that was catching on another metal piece that, in the normal way of things, it should not have been in contact with. [He was not a technical man.] As they parked up for the night, careful to avoid the raised concrete section of Wolf's driveway that he blamed for causing all the trouble in the first place, he knew already with a sinking heart that the car would not start in the morning.

MONDAY

It's hard to explain but I feel something momentous is happening here. I really do! I sense a shift in things, here on this sultry, unspoilt island that's a million miles from irony and sarcasm and small-minded Brits.

I genuinely believe that in healing ourselves, we can start to heal the planet. But I can't do it without you, Colleen. I need you by my side. You are my guiding light. You know this.

I. NOT THE ONLY JOKER ROUND HERE

First thing that morning, on the trail of groceries, Wolf drove himself and Andrew down a long bumpy track Andrew had never even spotted before, one that doubled round behind the house then wound along one side of a shallow old quarry before depositing them abruptly on the main road heading north. After a couple of miles, Wolf had gone cross-country again, inching along a sinuous farm track and emerging eventually by a busy roundabout with a decent-sized retail park attached to it.

Their conversation in the car had been friendly but functional. Wolf, who drove with the lazy efficiency of a man who knew the area like the back of his hand and – to Andrew's poorly concealed alarm – saw no need to look where he was going, discoursed on the possible problems with the car, assessing the relative probability of each scenario and outlining various remedies.

'But I just can't be sure!' he said again, beating the wheel in mock frustration. 'I'm going to have to get Tony onto it.'

Tony was Wolf's 'old mate'. He was the local car man. What Tony didn't know about cars was not worth knowing. Tony, indeed, had forgotten more about cars than the rest of us could ever hope to know. Wolf had already left him a message, and he had every hope that Tony might be able to pop round this evening.

'Thanks so much for all the help you've given us,' Andrew said for the umpty-seventh time. Like Colleen, he still felt a bit odd about calling his benefactor Wolf. [Interesting prefix, *umpty*. Must look it up.]

'Oh, think nothing of it, dear sir,' said Wolf, with that playful over-formality that seemed to be his default register. 'It's all part of the service.' He stroked the dog's muzzle. Jack was in the back, alternating between sniffing the rushing air out of a half-open window and resting his chin on his owner's shoulder.

'Well, it's very much appreciated, sir.' *Sir?* This mock formality of Wolf's was clearly infectious. It was fun, actually, a bit like role play. As an enthusiastic speaker of romance languages, Andrew was always chuffed to have an excuse to use the vocative case a bit more in English. One of his ambitions in life was to feel mature enough to be able to shout out 'Thank you, driver!' as he got off a bus, without a shred of irony either perceived or intended. Now *that* would be a real coming-of-age moment.

Wolf's accent was really quite unusual, Andrew thought. Just when you were sure he sounded German, out came something with a very Cornish lilt. But there was something else in there too, something that reminded Andrew of a well-spoken Dane he'd once met on a transcreation course in

Luxembourg. The Scandinavians spoke exceptional English, of course. Some of them, it seemed to him, had an accent that was actually more British than the British, perhaps because it was a pure theoretical pronunciation, untainted by any geographic filter. Perhaps, paradoxically, it was this impossible phonetic perfection that betrayed the speaker as a non-native. Anyway. Despite its unusual, unplaceable quality, Wolf's accent was quite euphonious, almost musical.

'So . . . Wolf. That's an unusual name?'

'Oh, it is and it isn't,' he replied, grimacing at the windscreen. 'My mother obviously didn't think so. You stupid animal!' he said tenderly to Jack, who had his chin back on Wolf's shoulder and was now attempting to lick his owner's ear.

Andrew was about to ask if *Wolf* was short for anything, or where his mother came from, but Wolf raised a sudden index finger and cut him short.

'Or my father, I should add!'

Andrew was silent for a moment. He was about to ask Wolf where his father came from, but Wolf got in first again.

'You know, it's a good idea to leave the light on in the en-suite if you go out,' he said. 'Then the fan can carry on clearing the air, if you've had a long shower. Or, you know, the other one.' He guffawed conspiratorially.

'Right,' said Andrew. Thinking of the morning's intense movement, he nodded again. '*Right.*'

In the supermarket, Andrew whizzed round with his trolley, desperate not to miss the arrival of the twins, while Wolf dawdled by the freezers, apparently intent on comparing every available size and make of white fish available, before finally plumping for a large economy bag of basa fillets, and two Fray Bentos pies of the old tinned sort that Andrew hadn't seen for years.

'A treat for Jack.' Wolf smiled. 'Cheap and cheerful. But for some reason he loves it!'

'So, fish for you and Mrs Wolf, tonight?' said Andrew, facilely.

Wolf frowned. 'No,' he said. 'The *pies* are for us.' He seemed genuinely confused, so Andrew hastened to assure him that he was joking.

At this, Wolf's features exploded into a delighted, wheezy snort. 'I know, I know!' he said, and Jack responded with a single bark. 'You are not the only joker round here, you know.'

Andrew laughed, a little.

'Here,' said Wolf. 'I got this for you.' He handed over a pack of camomile tea.

'Oh,' said Andrew. 'Thank you.'

'Not all, dear boy, not at all. A man in your condition needs to get a decent night's sleep.'

II. EVERY PROBLEM IS DOUBLE

'Grandaaaaaaaaaaaad!'

Sonja and the twins were early. Colleen and Andrew had followed their daughter and grandchildren's progress from Wales using the Find My Friends app, watching the blue dot move slowly along the big blue roads, then on to the yellow ones, the little red ones and finally the very little black ones.

Andrew had been in and out all morning with Wolf, picking up bits from the supermarket and trying to sort the car. They had plans to take the kids to the beach for the afternoon, but when Andrew tried to start the Astra, there was no joy, and he'd quickly flooded the engine.

No joy. That was one way of putting things.

She had once done a Basic Car Maintenance course at their local Adult Education place, run by a relentlessly patronising ex-driving instructor. Despite his primeval manner – 'nothing wrong with a big end in this game, ladies!' – she'd actually learned a lot, and could now do lots of basic stuff, including changing a tyre, something she was pretty sure Andrew wouldn't have a clue about. But this problem, whatever it was, looked above her pay grade. Not that she had been consulted.

Andrew's way of dealing with the issue, meanwhile, was to walk around acting all charming and ineffectual – not that tough an act for him, really – until someone who knew what they were doing took pity on him. Wolf in this case.

Wolf had insisted on looking under the car, opening up the bonnet and running through various drills and checks. As with the broadband, the boiler and everything else, he was energetic and practical, the man who knew. Jack ran non-stop around the car and the courtyard, shadowing his owner, desperate to help in some way.

She toyed with messaging Gerry again, whose latest texts had much to say about destiny and desire, not to mention healing the planet. But communicating with him set off a sort of aching confusion that made it hard to think about anything else. And just now, she wanted to think only about Billy and Ginny. Sonja too, obviously. But especially the twins.

She'd wanted to get some nice bits in for lunch, and Wolf had offered to drive Andrew to the nearest supermarket so he could pick up baguettes, sliced meat, fresh fruit juice, maybe a watermelon, as well as lots of sparkling water and the paper. (Sparkling water made non-alcoholic drinking a bit more interesting, she found. The bubbles gave your mouth a little edge, something to get a purchase on.) Wolf had one of those big half-car, half-truck things that looks like two different vehicles wedged together. When he revved the engine, it made the fruity roar that big motorbikes make, the sort of sound that rips the suburban air and leaves pedestrians cursing.

While they were gone, Colleen nipped round the side again. She called several times, but there was no response.

The little saucer of tuna she'd left out the night before had been mostly eaten, however, and the remains were attracting flies. As she picked the saucer up she wondered why she didn't want to tell Andrew about the cat.

The night had been uneventful, by their standards. Andrew had been up and about a bit, she sensed vaguely, but then he often was, what with his insomnia and her alleged snoring. (Though even if she did snore, it couldn't possibly be anything like as bad as his; he snored so loudly he probably woke *himself* up, which may be what caused his insomnia in the first place.) She had stayed up reading for a while herself, drinking a hot chocolate made with a Cadbury's sachet she found in the kitchen cupboard and racing through the best bits of *My Mother the Psychopath* and *Murder at 40 Below: True Crime Stories from Alaska*, after which she eventually dropped off into a long and deep sleep.

Andrew was standing at the edge of the drive, all signs of sleeplessness gone, making sure to direct Sonja's car past the offending bit of concrete that had damaged their Astra. (She saw now that the thing they'd hit was like a little traffic island, designed to divide the driveway, so that cars were naturally directed either towards the Wolf house or round into their cottage courtyard. It was perfectly missable if you knew it was there, in daylight at least. Wolf said it was also mentioned in the bumf about the cottage and on the website.)

At the sight of the twins, her husband was in high silly mode already, prancing around and waving his arms like one of those men in earplugs at airports who steer planes with table-tennis bats. She felt a flutter of excitement and for no reason checked her hair in the hall mirror. Her throat felt dry and there was a dull thudding in her head; she must have drunk too much coffee. The family all together. The twins. Sonja . . . She felt again that uncomfortable mix of joy and panic.

She saw through the window the familiar white car. A snazzy-looking, 4WD thing, something Japanese, with screens in the back for the kids. No sign of Simon, of course, she knew that already. He was away on another of his trips, negotiating shipping contracts in Brazil or Saudi or somewhere. (She had casually asked a few of her high-end clients about the law firm Simon was a partner in; it had a reputation for 'getting results in difficult countries', they told her, whatever that meant. They also confirmed that its fees were reassuringly expensive.)

Billy and Ginny were out of the car already, dancing around Andrew. She could hear Jack barking from the house. And now, she didn't quite remember how, she was out there with them, the familiar pangs swallowed in the joyous anarchy of young children. Now she was hugging and kissing and dancing – they were young to be grandparents, after all – and before she knew it they were all up on the meadow, throwing a frisbee that had appeared from somewhere and kicking a rugby ball (ditto) and making daisy chains and filling buckets with acorns and seed pods.

From a high side window of Wolf's house she saw the face of an elderly woman, hair in curlers, grinning and waving. Colleen pointed her out to the children and they all waved back.

She gestured to the woman to come on down and join them, but the woman just kept on smiling and waving. The exchange started to get a bit awkward; in the end Colleen took advantage of a tennis ball that had rolled suddenly up to her feet. She gave a final wave and a sort of friendly *if-you-can't-beat-'em* shrug, picked up the ball and ran off towards the action.

When she turned back a few moments later, the woman was no longer at the window.

Andrew and Sonja brought out cups of tea for the adults, and glasses of milk and mini Twix bars for the little ones.

Father and daughter stood chatting at the meadow gate, looking on as Colleen danced and ran about with the twins. They were talking in low tones, she noticed, with the unmistakable air of two people trying to look like they were *not* trying to avoid being overheard.

She knew what they were talking about. Who.

But now Andrew, sensing her watching him, had put his mug down, the one that bore the legend, 'If it involves a series of unexplained corpses, count me in'. (Her mug also had a quote on it: 'If you can't beat 'em, eat 'em', next to a picture of a meat cleaver.) Andrew was back out on the grass now, tag-teaming the fun with her, so that she could take her turn standing with Sonja, getting her breath back and sipping from her true-crime mug, while her husband cavorted like a nincompoop.

At Andrew's reappearance on the scene, the children's excitement and giggling stepped up a notch. He was a very good nincompoop, and his silliness was infectious. Soon they were all watching and laughing as he imitated a series of animals and inanimate objects – a giraffe, a flipflop, a ham croissant.

'So . . . how are you?'

Sonja looked her straight in the eyes, frank and direct. She was her daughter all right.

'Good, good. This week has been a tonic.' She didn't know why she said that, or what it meant. 'And what about you? Managing without Simon?'

She hadn't meant it to, but it came out as a bit of a taunt. Simon almost never came to see them. He always had too much on, another client meeting, another business trip to somewhere dodgy.

'He's good. We're good. After this one he's going to get a decent bit of time off.'

'That's *great*,' Colleen said warmly. 'And how are the kids?'

'Oh, they're grand,' said Sonja. 'Having them in pre-school makes a huge difference.'

'I bet. Must give you a bit of breathing space.'

'Most of the time they get on. But it's just . . . you know, every problem is double? And of course they know just how to push each other's buttons. If one can't sleep, they end up waking the other. Every problem comes in twos . . .' She paused, and nodded quickly in succession at her mum and then over at her dad. 'But of course you two know all this . . .'

Colleen scrunched her eyes and looked inscrutably over the field. She was suddenly very thirsty.

Sonja put a hand on hers; she flinched slightly in response, but kept hers there. She looked at her daughter, met her gaze. Sonja was tall and thin, as she'd always been, with very light blonde hair and that permanent expression of kindliness that Colleen had always worried would be taken advantage of. She was a natural mum, but despite appearances she wasn't a pushover: she had a real backbone, and if she thought something was out of order, you'd soon know about it.

'How are you two doing? Really?'

'We're . . . doing OK. This week's been a . . .'

'A tonic?' said Sonja, smiling.

'The oven!' said Colleen suddenly. 'I've left the chicken nuggets on. And the chips!'

'I'll come with you. Give you a hand.'

'No, love, you're OK,' said Colleen. 'You stay with the kids. I'll call when the food's done.'

Aware that her daughter was tracking her course, Colleen ran across the gravel and found sanctuary behind the kitchen blinds, where she opened a big bag of oven chips and another of nuggets, spread them out on baking trays and set them to cook in the oven that Andrew must have already set to pre-heat. *What a team!*

She looked out of the window and saw that the others were all still up on the meadow. She slipped into the utility room, opened up the cupboard next to the tumble dryer and carefully pushed the oven spray and fabric conditioner to one side to check what lay behind.

There were two of them, as expected, lying side by side. Peas in a pod. Twins. Distinctive bottles, with the stocky glass body, stubby silver lids, and fancy handwriting on the label. Something about being imported. In thick blue block capitals, she made out the word ABSOLUT.

As she was tidying up, her eye was drawn through the glass door to a sudden little movement. It seemed to come from a bag of clothes pegs that she could see hanging on a revolving dryer in the garden. There was something about the way the green bag hung heavily, the way its body sagged and its mouth bulged. Moving to the door, she saw through the pane what had fallen, saw two more of them on the ground already, and laughed a quiet bitter laugh.

She went outside and picked the items up. She pocketed them, then went to inspect the peg bag. At a rough count, it contained a good dozen more Jack Daniels miniatures. She felt something brush against her ankles. The little black cat was back, bolder now, weaving slinky figures of eight about her legs.

'You bloody nincompoop,' she said out loud, feeling deliriously happy and bitterly sad as the ironies swirled about her.

III. DONKEY-PIRATE-CHASE

Sitting on the loo, sneaking a quick breather from the grandkids, Andrew flicked through stuff on his phone. He had a sudden need to confirm whether a *Malteser* really was a term for a person of or from Malta. It was the sort of thing people expected him to know, and he was impatient to fill the gap.

Soon enough, he found a Malta travel website with an article entitled: 'Are people from Malta really known as Maltesers?'

FALSE, said the article quite emphatically. There was no relation, Andrew read, between the confectionery and the people of Malta or their country. The name Malteser was apparently a portmanteau of *malt* – a principal ingredient of the sweet – and *teaser*, perhaps because the product teases the tongue with its pleasing chocolate-coated honeycomb mouth-feel? [Good word, *mouthfeel*. Something very German in its morphology.] 'Having said all that,' the article added wearily, 'we've never met a Maltese person who's visited Australia, Canada, the US or the British Isles without being teased about being a Malteser!'

Portmanteau words. Another area of interest. Everyone knew about *labradoodle* and *liger* and *jeggings*, of course, but who remembered these days that *chortle* was actually a Carrollian blend of *chuckle* and *snort*? Or that *hassle* was really originally *haggle* + *tussle* [probably, according to Oxford anyway].

The hassle of the broken-down car had dragged on that morning, and he felt awful that Wolf had gone to so much trouble on their behalf, with so little to show for it. The actual scraping of the underside of the car was probably not the problem, Wolf concluded, unless the transmission had been damaged or there was an issue with the U-joint of the prop shaft. Alternatively, however, it could be that the prang had set off another problem that would have emerged sooner or later, something related to the gasket or to longer-term steerage linkage wear.

Every scenario Wolf painted was as plausible to Andrew as it was impenetrable. The irony of all this was not lost on Andrew, a mechanical illiterate who made a living from translating marketing messages written by one set of people into a language that another set could understand. [Strictly the word for what he did was *transcreation*, of course. As he liked to explain, 'I render the marketing as well as the message – the *sizzle* as well as the sausage.']

So what was the condition that Wolf thought he was in? Exhaustion, he speculated, from his sanctuary in the pine-scented loo. Did Wolf see him up at night? He certainly saw Wolf.

'Grandaaaaaad? Are you coming? Come and make a den with us!'

Ginny and Billy were banging mercilessly at the loo door. They delighted him, of course they did. But his earlier romping around the meadow had left him shattered – the long baffling session of donkey-pirate-chase [a game of fluid rules, one of the twins' own inventions, with frenzied chasing of Grandad the one constant], followed by the frisbee version of piggy in the middle [spoiler: Grandad is *always* the piggie], followed by the numerous rounds of forty:forty. [How incidentally would one write *forty:forty*? As words or ordinals? With a colon or a hyphen, or nothing? Yet another thing to look up . . .] Andrew felt winded and a little nauseous; since the twins' arrival, he noted with breathless satisfaction, his step count for the day had risen by over 3700 already.

Then there was the sadness.

Here they were, all together. And yet they were not complete, not really . . . *quorate*. [Quartate?] Ned hadn't messaged for a good twelve hours, not since the latest money transfer, which Andrew took as good news, if only temporarily. Unless of course it was very, very bad news, so bad that Ned couldn't even send a desperate message about it. Either way, there was nothing he could do about it, except worry.

'Andrew, love, are you in there?'

Love, eh? Blimey. There was nothing like the twins to put Colleen in a good mood.

'Just coming, love!' he called back, as cheerily as poss.

He gave his emails a last flick, and wished at once that he hadn't. There it was again.

We wish we didn't have to send this

It got your attention, every single time. He couldn't help catching the first line of the message in the preview pane:

Dear Andrew and Colleen, this is the hardest email we've ever had to send . . .

He hit delete, and laughed mirthlessly to himself, because deleting it did nothing. Not when you knew the whole thing off by heart anyway.

IV. AGE-INAPPROPRIATE

Mrs Wolf's earlier reluctance to come out to play was easily explained when she appeared now, hobbling across the gravel towards the meadow with the support of a stick. Wolf followed close behind her, watchful but not too close, pushing a wheelchair with a bulging plastic bag hanging from one of its handles.

'Hey, guys!' Colleen called to Billy and Ginny. 'Come and say hello to . . . *Mrs Wolf?*' Colleen turned hopelessly for confirmation to the new arrival.

'Oh no, dear,' said Mrs Wolf. 'Call me Hildy, please.'

The first thing that struck Colleen about Hildy (Hildi?) was that she looked like a parody of late-era Princess Margaret. She wore dark glasses and a pinkish tweedy two-piece, teamed with white court shoes. She sported bright pink lipstick and an elegant *coiffure*, her hair all tucked up high in a silken scarf. Though she was obviously of a similar age to Wolf (mid-seventies?), she now looked young for her age. It was a dramatic transformation that she had engineered since appearing as a face at the window before lunch.

'So now everyone, we are all here!' Wolf beamed from his position behind the empty chair. 'Or nearly, anyway.' He nodded towards Andrew, who was sneaking a look at his phone.

'Shut that dog up!' Mrs Wolf snarled with unexpected vehemence as Jack started barking loudly from behind the little wicker gate in front of the big house. Wolf raised an arm and pointed at Jack, who obediently lay down by the front door.

'He can come out to play, can't he?' asked Colleen. 'The children would love to meet him, I'm sure.'

'Oh dear me, no, love,' said Mrs Wolf. 'I'd never forgive myself. Not after Jilly.'

Colleen looked at Andrew, and knew at once that neither of them felt up to asking about Jilly.

'Perhaps tomorrow, when he's got to know them a bit better,' said Wolf from behind her. 'He'll have calmed down by then.'

The children, who were highly skilled already in the protocols of adult gift-giving, had obediently come over to say hello, compliantly offering the tops of their heads for pats and pecks and answering Hildy's questions with polite nods and even the odd syllable. Now, duties despatched, they stood expectantly by the meadow gate.

The questions, mind you, were of a sort you were unlikely to hear at the pre-school doorway.

'You're a handsome one!' Hildy said to Billy, clutching his chin a little too tightly. 'Got a girlfriend yet, dear? Treat her mean, do you?'

'Er, no,' said Billy, looking a bit flustered.

'And look at you, you saucy strumpet. Look at those legs!' said Hildy to Ginny. 'I bet you're a terrible flirt, aren't you? Flash 'em a bit of what they're missing, do you?' She turned and cackled at Wolf, who smiled quietly, as if to himself. Though her manner was grand, her voice was pure West Country.

Colleen was startled. It was really unusual to hear an adult speaking inappropriately to a child these days. When she was growing up, such dodgy exchanges were far more common (and here briefly she was seized by a not-very-pleasant memory of a certain unofficial 'uncle'). Hildy's questions were shocking and yet somehow familiar.

'Wolf!' she called. 'The bag!'

Wolf quickly darted forward with the bag from the wheelchair, and Hildy rested one stick on the gate so she could rummage inside.

'This stupid hip!' she said confidentially to Colleen. 'It holds me back so much! I can't wait to get back on my feet.'

'Did you have . . . an op?' ventured Colleen.

'Walking again in three weeks, they said!' said Hildy. 'Just look at me.'

'Mrs Wolf is making excellent progress,' said Wolf. 'We're very proud of her.'

'My name is *Hildy*, Wolf,' she scolded, with a despairing shake of her head for Colleen's benefit and a look that said: *Men, eh?*

Billy and Ginny held out their hands as Hildy took a couple of faltering steps towards them. Jack was standing at the gate now, eyeing her closely.

'Come on, you two! You come to Hildy! Make it easier for her.'

They rounded the meadow gate and eagerly took receipt of a wrapped item each, then in turn gave Hildy an awkward hug around the waist.

Ginny unwrapped hers where she stood, sensing that sharing the spectacle of her delighted response was the final tax she owed the adults for their generosity. Billy, meanwhile, had run off with his present into the corner of the meadow, like a nervous kitten anxious to keep his treasured morsel away from a cunning sibling.

The presents, Colleen noted, were both rather expensive and strikingly ill-suited to their recipients. Billy got an Airfix kit of a Sunderland flying boat, which even the box said was for children 11-plus. Ginny got an embroidery kit aimed at sewing enthusiasts nearly three times her age.

'Thank you!' the children trilled politely, depositing their presents with Colleen and running off to play donkey-pirate-chase with Grandad again. The adults all smiled at each other politely. Everyone knew, Colleen assumed, that it was a bad sign if they gave the pressies straight back like that.

Colleen's heart sank further when she scanned the contents of the sewing set, which included an 'easy headband project' and the chance to learn a dozen kinds of stitch. All the bits – needles, threads, buttons, embroidery hoop, thimbles, felt shapes, tracing paper and more – came in 'a delightful butterfly-shaped metallic keepsake container that children will want to use to keep all their future embroidery things together!'

There's goes my evening, thought Colleen, who was actually quite good at sewing, thanks to a mum who had zealously insisted on teaching her such 'life skills'. She smiled at the memory. Her mum had been a pain with all her self-improvement lessons, but she had plugged away despite her daughter's suspicion that mastery of cross-stitch, macramé, basic ballroom-dance steps and pickling were not perhaps as essential to a self-reliant twenty-first-century life as they might once have been. In later life, however, Colleen had discovered that others found a certain vintage charm in her talents. Being able to gut a mackerel or grow a plant from a cutting or make a béchamel sauce from scratch . . . to contemporary friends and lovers, these obscure old-school hacks were quaint party pieces, to be shown off with ironic pride, a bit like being able to do proper shorthand or blow a half-decent tune on the sax.

'How many can we have, Granny? How many?'

Now the children were dancing around her again – and they caused her a moment's confusion till she remembered who they meant by *Granny*; she still found it odd to be called that. She saw that Wolf and Hildy had supplemented their initial, age-inappropriate gifts with a gigantic bag full of lots of little packs of Haribo sweets, and all was well again in the little ones' world.

'Lunchtime!' called Andrew from the kitchen, and after issuing another batch of thank yous to the older couple – more exhausting gratefulness! – Colleen led the children off to their cottage.

'Bye, Jack! Bye!' trilled the children, and the dog wagged his tail and panted happily back at them.

As Colleen was about to go inside, Wolf came striding over. 'Don't forget the toys in the cupboard,' he chirped. 'For the little ones.'

'I won't,' said Colleen. 'And thank you again,' she added helplessly.

'Actually,' said Wolf, coming rather close now, so close she could make out a couple of little patches of worn eczematic skin on his pate. 'It is I who should be thanking you.'

'Oh, don't be silly,' said Colleen reflexively. And then, not able to help herself, and perhaps relieved at not having to be doing all the thanking for once, she added, 'How do you mean?'

'Mrs Wolf,' said Wolf. 'That's the first time she's left the house. In three months.'

'What, since the op?'

'Ah. Yes. The "op".' Wolf turned the word over experimentally, deploying his thin, elegant hands to put big dramatic scare quotes around it. 'Yes. One could say that.'

Colleen always knew when a client wanted her to prod further.

'You *could* say that?' she repeated. 'You mean . . .'

'Well, you know . . .' he said quickly, and then paused. He stood silent for a time, picking with quiet methodical obsessiveness at a thin line of moss that had insinuated itself between two rows of bricks. At last he added, 'The op is more a state of mind than a single event, if you know what I mean.'

'Oh,' said Colleen. 'Yes. I think I do.'

'I'm sure you do,' he replied, with a twinkle.

'She looked very smart today.'

He looked pleased. 'Yes, she did.' He smiled fondly. 'She dressed up like that for your benefit.' Here he extended his arms to take in all the current inhabitants of the cottage. 'First time in ages.'

'I'm glad,' said Colleen simply.

Wolf turned away, and then abruptly turned back. 'Oh, and by the way,' he said. 'You should always wear blue.'

'Really?' said Colleen, patting her hair.

'Yes! Definitely!' he replied. 'It suits your eyes. Makes you look so pretty!'

'Oh,' said Colleen, quite disarmed. '*Thank* you.'

'Yes!' he added. 'So much *younger.*'

V. MR MCGREGOR'S GARDEN

Days with little children were long, Andrew was remembering. Their energy was insatiable, as was their hunger for attention [and for Haribos, given half a chance].

After lunch and a few rounds of hide-and-seek in the house, Andrew set the kids up with *Finding Nemo* on the big telly — the story, he couldn't help noticing again, of a dad trying to get his son back – so that the grown-ups could all sit round the kitchen table with a nice cup of tea and a slice of Hildy's sponge cake. A well-earned breather.

'I'm sorry, we'll all have to make do with Earl Grey,' said Colleen. 'That's all they've got in the place. I forgot to bring the PG Tips.'

'Or the Yorkshire,' said Andrew, predictably. Their war over tea preferences had been quietly rumbling for about twenty years.

As Colleen busied herself with the cups and plates, Sonja studied the Saturday crossword. Andrew had spent years schooling her in the ways of the cryptics, teaching her the arcane code that lay behind this obscure outpost of Britishness, a code that to this day – and quite unnecessarily really – could only really be broken by someone with a knowledge of cricket, CoE clergy and a whole gamut of obscure initialisms.

She quickly solved one, and Andrew kicked himself. Even before she said it, he somehow instantly knew that 'Universe of a hundred thousand broken bones' was COSMOS. But he said nothing, and smiled warmly, savouring his daughter's triumph.

'See what you think about 17 across. The wedding transport one.'

'You know it, do you?'

'I have an idea. But your mum's still working on it.' This came out wrong.

'Oooh! *clever-clever-clever*,' said Colleen from over by the kettle.

He closed his eyes and his mouth went very, very straight. Clearly, he had a gift for saying the wrong thing, while *she* had a gift for taking things the wrong way. It was the perfect combination. Perfect as in *perfect storm*.

They talked about this and that, nattered about Simon's job, Sonja's imminent return to teaching [part-time, to start with], and the emerging personalities and differences in the two twins. Ginny was the outgoing, responsible one, though she had a strong will and was not to be crossed.

'Like someone else I know.' Colleen smiled meaningfully at her daughter.

The boy, on the other hand, was more secretive, kept his feelings to himself. 'He's good at sport,' said Andrew. 'And he's a crafty one. I reckon Ned's going to be a real joker.'

Colleen looked at him sharply.

'Ned?' said Sonja.

'Oh. Sorry, sorry. I meant Billy. Obviously.' Andrew felt his face burning.

Sonja looked down to a floor that was suddenly littered with eggshells. 'I don't suppose you've heard from . . .'

Now Colleen looked sharply at Sonja, daring her to continue.

'From . . . my brother.'

Colleen glared at her. Sonja looked back. The question was out there now and, Andrew noted with quiet pride [very quiet pride], his daughter would not look away, however uncomfortable she must be feeling.

Colleen now looked hard at Andrew, as if accusing him of having put their daughter up to this . . . blasphemy. And then she looked at the crossword, at her cup, at her hands.

The silence that followed was punctuated only by the ticking of the kitchen clock for a while, and then – blessedly – by Wolf whistling as he strode about the courtyard, opening up the bonnet of their car and poking about in the engine with great purpose.

'I . . . I gave him the keys,' said Andrew.

After that things picked up again, a bit, as they turned back to the shallows to discuss safer topics: troubles with the car, the local roads [very narrow!] and the comedy of the crappy village shop. But the conversation had a mournful, winded quality now, and every willing canter petered out into listless silence.

'Grandaaaaaaaaaaaaad! Let's play donkey-pirate-chase!'

The children had emerged from the next room. They'd already had enough of the whole missing-fish-son thing, well before the end, well before the exciting bit where Nemo gets put in the fish tank in the dental surgery and the big bird does its rescue, and Nemo goes down the sewer and . . . and anyway, Andrew realised he was suddenly actually very relieved to see them both, and delighted to have an excuse to be away from the kitchen table and up on his feet and out the door and roaming around the steep landscaped terraces of their own little wrap-around garden – steering well clear of the clothes washer and its peg bag, of course, though he was pleased to see that all was in order there – and just being silly again, getting sweaty and breathless, and basically feeling too knackered to be able to think about other stuff.

Certainly he wasn't thinking that much when Billy threw the rugby ball over the fence into the back of Wolf's garden, and Andrew eased his legs over and into the vegetable patch to retrieve it. He had a sudden image of Benjamin Bunny straying into Mr McGregor's lettuces, but then again Wolf had been so ridiculously accommodating it was impossible to imagine that he would mind this small intrusion in the slightest. He could even imagine Wolf beckoning him over the fence.

As he leant over a cloche to extricate the ball from between two expertly raised lines of fine dark earth, careful not to disturb a large, rather chewed-up dog bone, Andrew was momentarily dazzled by the glint of sun reflected by the window of a large outhouse. He peered in, expecting to be charmed by the usual jumble of potting-shed paraphernalia.

It wasn't, in fact, much of a shed at all. It was more like a trading desk or a recording studio. There were a couple of monitors on one side, next to some sort of control deck full of sliding buttons and complicated-looking dials. On another surface, at the back of the shed, there was a jumble of electronic kit: Andrew was no expert in such things, but he made out various speakers and some mics. There was a jumble of wires, a rack of delicate screwdrivers, and various bits of kit that had been opened up and were obviously being worked on in some way. A pair of fancy-looking headphones was carefully draped over the back of a revolving chair.

Wolf must be some sort of amateur short-wave radio ham, thought Andrew, his mind irresistibly if irrelevantly drawn to dim memories of CB radio geeks, Kris Kristofferson in *Convoy* [or was that Burt Reynolds? Ooh, Ali MacGraw . . .] Rubber Duck, and '10-10 till we do it again!'

I bet he's a metal detectorist on the side too.

Andrew thought, in fact, that Wolf was still out the front in the courtyard, tinkering with his guests' car. So it was something of a surprise to catch a glimpse of him through the nearest window of the big house. The window looked down into the room, a sort of sunken scullery with a big dresser and a double set of Butler sinks, where Andrew was even more surprised to glimpse Wolf cowering on the tiled floor in front of his wife, who was up on her feet and – in what was perhaps the biggest surprise of all – appeared to be flogging her spouse with some sort of leather strap. Jack sat to attention by his master's recumbent form, eyeing Mrs Wolf with awe.

Then Peter Rabbit gathered up his little bunnies and ran all the way home, where he ate a lovely lamb stew washed down with fizzy water, and had to wait till the wee ones were all tucked up safely in bed before he told the story of Mr and Mrs pervy Wolf to his disbelieving wife and daughter.

VI. DON'T WAKE THE KIDS

'I *still* can't believe you saw that,' said Colleen, undressing. 'Are you really sure?'

Andrew put on his best cod Nazi/West Country mash-up accent. 'My dear laydeee! I saw vat I saw.'

'Do you think . . . ? I mean, could he be a war criminal?'

Andrew snorted with mirth. Colleen giggled too. They had quite recently watched *The Boys from Brazil* for the first time in years, though both had dropped off before the end.

'Ssshhh! Don't wake the kids! I mean, that's about seven kinds of racism . . . though I do sort of know what you mean,' he whispered back. 'But the years don't exactly tally, do they?'

'How do you mean?'

'Well, if Wolf was a Nazi he'd be about a hundred now, wouldn't he?'

'But it would explain why he lets her hit him.'

'How so?'

'Well . . .' Her eyes twinkled as she applied a brush to her nails. 'Let's say he's done some terrible thing that can never be forgiven. But every day he does his penance, with the help of Mrs W.'

'Huh! Maybe he's a mass murderer who's never been brought to justice?'

'Oooh, yes. That would explain the obsession with true-crime books.' He was sitting next to her on the bed now. She felt a heat between their skins, felt a gently urgent tugging in her stomach.

'Yes!' They were both enjoying this. 'Perhaps the beatings are just enough to help him get through the night. Help him . . . live with the guilt. Maybe get some sleep.'

'I'm not sure he sleeps that much,' said Andrew, reminding her that he'd seen Wolf's face at the window in the small hours, seen lights go on and off at all sorts of odd times.

The mystery of the Wolfs had been the topic of choice for most of the evening, once the kids were bathed and tucked up in bed, and Andrew and Colleen each read them a story.

Colleen found a copy of *Mr Gumpy's Outing* on one of the shelves in the bedroom. It had been one of her own favourites when Sonja was growing up. Mr Gumpy lives in a lovely big ramshackle house by the river. He has a punt. One by one, a succession of animals ask if they can join him on his boat trip. To each, Mr Gumpy says yes but adds a specific caveat. *So long as you don't squawk/bleat/flap about . . .* etc.

In the event, all the animals – plus two children – pile into the boat. Every single animal, of course, does the exact thing that Mr Gumpy has asked them not to do. As a result, the boat capsizes and they all fall into the river with an almighty splash.

But the real charm of the story – along with the incredible green washed-out illustrations, which perfectly convey a truly sultry day – is that everyone gets out, dries off and heads to Mr Gumpy's for a slap-up tea. No fuss, no recriminations, no judgement. And at the end, Mr Gumpy – who, contrary to what you might expect, is not at all *grumpy*, quite the opposite – kindly asks everyone to come back again, another day. Mr Gumpy was a bit like Wolf, she decided.

It was a story, she supposed, about unconditional love, and acceptance. If only life were that simple. If only that was how to fix stuff.

After that, Andrew read a rather unsatisfactory story about some superhero characters made of Lego. And then, what with all the excitement of the day and the car journey and the running around, the twins went off to sleep quite easily.

There was a moment, just a moment, when she stood with her husband at the bedroom door, and they looked together over at those two adorable heads sunken into soft pillows, side by side in their twin beds, and it was just like they had once stood and looked over at their own two, a lifetime ago.

Sonja thought the whole Wolf thing was hilarious. She was convinced it was a sexual thing, and the idea of pensioners doing S&M seemed to tickle her funny bone in a way that her mum found slightly disconcerting.

Though her parents thought of Sonja as practical and responsible, they were dimly aware of a more risqué side to her character. Doubtless they were the last people who were ever supposed to see this, let alone understand it; they just caught the odd glimpse of it from the occasional remark Ned used to make about 'Sonja's insatiable libido', the things that made her laugh on telly, the books in her room.

Colleen still grimaced at the memory of the time she stayed over with Sonja in her old flat, back in the pre-Simon days. Casting around for something to read, she picked up an intriguing paperback with a shiny cover. It turned out to be called *The Orgasmic Threesome*. Colleen had arched an eyebrow and quipped that she couldn't imagine a novel with a title like that winning the Booker. There followed an awkward moment when Colleen realised that the book wasn't in fact a work of fiction at all, but actually a sort of self-help book; and then there was an even more awkward silence as she realised that her daughter now realised that her mum had just realised this too.

The other clue to this side of Sonja was of course the figure of Simon himself. He had a decadent, louche sort of look, and if Sonja said she'd met him at an orgy her mum wouldn't have been surprised. (Andrew's nickname for him was 'Lord Henry', after a character in, was it, *Dorian Gray?*) Simon liked to make 'daring' puns in front of Andrew and Colleen and the kids about how he could 'really do with a spot of Coke'. Sonja would smirk nervously, caught between the rival claims of parents and husband, and Colleen wanted to shake him by the throat and say: 'I may be in my late forties but I've been to drama school, laddie! I know more about drugs than you ever will.' But of course, Sonja didn't know much about this side of her mum either.

'He's quite a character, Wolf, isn't he?' said Colleen now, rubbing in some hand cream and looking around for her reading glasses.

'And very thoughtful, in his way,' replied Andrew, passing her her specs.

'When he's not in the throes of one of his sexual punishment beatings, you mean.' This thing had a life of its own.

'Yes! Did you know he bought me a packet of camomile tea? To help me sleep, I think.'

'And the hours he's put in on that car . . . It's so above and beyond, it's almost too much.'

'Shame the car still doesn't start though.' They both giggled furtively, mindful of Sonja and the twins. Having to laugh under their breaths made everything twice as funny.

'I did ask if we could borrow *his* car,' said Andrew now. 'Get out for a day perhaps.'

'Ooh, good idea. What did he say?'

'He said the gearbox was very temperamental. But he'd gladly drive us both anywhere we want to go.'

'Oh God, we can't possibly ask that of him.'

'No, I know. Perhaps he knows that too. There's something almost *tyrannical* about his extreme kindness.'

'Mmm, or masochistic? That's it! Maybe he's deliberately *not* fixing the car . . . so his wife can punish him for his incompetence?'

'Yes! And that Tony. What's he? The dungeon master?'

More breathy giggling.

'Shame he didn't show up, though. We are going to need the car at some point.'

'Really? What on earth for?'

'What?' said Andrew, missing her sarcasm. 'Of course we will! We'll need to go *somewhere* at some point. Like home?'

'Why on earth would you possibly want to be anywhere but here? We've got the Forest of Deadly Quicksand on one side, and a load of ploughed fields on the other. Our neighbours are geriatric perverts. And if you need Tesco, it's just a quick yomp through five miles of abandoned tin mines.' They giggled some more.

Andrew put a hand on her calf, massaging the muscle like he used to. She sensed both uncertainty and great need in the gesture, and this moved her.

They kissed. She felt him as he pushed against her, trying – not so subtly – to ease them backwards onto the bed.

She kissed him back, hard, and then pulled away. In the distance, they heard Jack barking.

'Ssssssssh, we can't tonight,' she said. 'We've got the twins next door.'

He nodded dumbly.

'Do you want to lick my fingers?' she said, with a twinkle.

Andrew leant in, closed his eyes, and began licking.

'Oh! I was only joking!' She pulled her hand away. 'I put this yucky stuff on to help me stop biting my nails.'

He gagged a little, and she couldn't help giggling. But then she caught the look on his face as he tried to hide his hurt. She kissed him once more, tenderly, gliding a hand over his knee. 'Tomorrow, I promise.'

He sat up and adjusted his glasses. She could tell he was making a great effort.

'No. Of course,' he said, picking up his phone. 'I think I'll have a quick shower.'

She thought: *I do still want him. Sometimes. How much easier if I didn't.*

She nearly called after him, but the right words wouldn't come. And besides, how would it be tomorrow?

She had wanted to, tonight, she really had. More than the previous night. But to go back to the sex thing now would be to just pretend that everything was all right. And what, really, had changed?

He was still the man who had failed her when it mattered most.

He was still the man who had lost her son.

VII. FREEDOM FROM DESIRE

In the en-suite, with the shower on, Andrew flicked through some images on his phone and thought about doing the necessary.

But though he was sorely tempted, he noted that his frustration had an unexpected anticipatory quality. He felt excited for once, rather than the usual pinched and thwarted resentment. He could feel Colleen's warm, soft lips still. She had said *tomorrow*, hadn't she? He could wait another night, couldn't he? Honour her promise?

Yes. Why not. It would be sort of chivalric.

Quickly he finished his ablutions, brushing and flossing with the self-congratulatory solemnity of a lifelong ascetic. 'The inner freedom from the practical desire.' Ah, Eliot and St John of the Cross and the *via negativa* and all that.

There are insomniacs who cannot fall asleep, and others who fall asleep but wake up much too early and can't get off again. Andrew tended to fall into the former category, but he had done a bit of both. And anyway, he wasn't really an insomniac; he was just a man who stayed up waiting for messages from his wayward son.

leg really bad dad
like the other one

Another night, another transfer. More random banking; more random barking. Though he and Colleen had separate bank accounts [along with a joint one for bills], the holes were expanding and his cooking of the books was getting more creatively audacious by the day. It didn't help his earning potential that he was so often exhausted by his nights that he could barely function during his daytimes.

It might have been easier if Andrew didn't know what Ned's world was like. But he had been there a couple of times, descended thither from his soigné suburban domain, with its tennis courts and its Cook shop and its beauty salons, and seen at first hand the mean streets that Ned walked every day. [Good word, *thither.*]

He remembered the unlit walkways, the menacing groups of young men, the snarling dogs. The undercurrent of violence, the feeling that anything could happen and no one would give a toss. To his own shame, Andrew had not really understood that such places existed in his own city, let alone just a couple of miles from his house. He had brought Ned money a couple of times, and once had to pay off a debt and make a purchase on his son's behalf. He wouldn't forget that in a hurry. The fortified entrance. A knife in his face. Terrifying stunted men with yellow skin. A spider's web tattoo across a pitiless face.

Afterwards he tried to congratulate himself on his 'courage', on a job well done; soon after that, he had found himself weeping with relief at still being alive. Ned had taken the stuff and disappeared into the night, no time to discuss the footie or even say thanks.

He didn't do it for the thanks, of course. He did it because he didn't know how not to.

Back in bed, he dared slip an arm around Colleen, and was rewarded with a quiet squeezed acceptance of the gesture. He stretched out his legs, a foot of his hooked under a foot on hers, like they always used to, and tucked into *The True Story of the Manson Murders.*

These books were addictive, but he found that a couple of chapters of each was enough. Typically, the first few sections would outline the atrocities committed, and sketch out the appalling yet fascinating character of the psychopath; after devouring these bits, he found he was ready to move on to the next book. He didn't hang around to see the detail of how the crime was solved, how the criminal mastermind was brought to justice. The Psychos, let's face it, are always more compelling than the Plods. And outside of cryptic crosswords, he was suspicious of solutions.

That night he had a dream about Wolf. Wolf was a mass murderer, albeit a courteous one, but his wife was very cross about his crimes. She took him into a shed and applied electrodes to his bits. The howling of Wolf ended the dream, but in the way of dreams this coincided with the start of his realisation that there was howling outside. Foxes mating in the woods, no doubt. Sex was torture for animals too.

Andrew carefully disentangled himself from Colleen's arm – most unusually, they had been sleeping entwined – and pulled back the curtain a little, just enough to look across at the big house. All was silent and black. Out here the stars were incredible, like a sky from the Bible.

Andrew's gaze panned across to Mr McGregor's outhouse. He made out the shape of a seated figure, his face intermittently visible in the reflection of a flickering screen.

'Oh well,' he said out loud. 'At least she didn't kill him.'

TUESDAY

I'll be the first to admit that we'd had a few ourselves. We have to, when we go out with you two, just to get through the night.

But when the manager came over and asked us to leave, me and Paul sobered right up. And as we left, I actually heard some of the other customers cheering and clapping.

I. NED DEAD

Ginny and Billy greeted the day with a running jump onto Granny and Grandad's bed. Colleen and Andrew were jolted rudely awake, quite seriously winded, and tickled pink, all at once. How could you not be, when these perfect little people climbed in under the duvet and snuggled up against you with their warm bodies and their unthinking affection and their wondrous questions?

'*Are you thinking about my jeggings, Granny?*'

'*Why is your face so red, Grandad?*'

'*When will you die?*'

'*Where is Uncle Ned?*'

'Ned's in bed!' said Ginny, his twin sister, and giggled. 'He's always in bed.'

'Ned dead! Ned dead!' replied Billy, innocently seduced by rhyme.

Colleen excused herself to head off to the bathroom, leaving Grandad to field the twins' questioning.

'No, of course not, Billy!' she heard him say. 'He's just . . . not been very well.' *Yeah, right. And whose fault is that?*

Their twins had been close as kids but had drifted apart in later years. To Colleen's knowledge, Ned had only met Sonja's twins once, at their christening. But then again, he may well have turned up on his sister's doorstep any number of times after that, desperate for funds or somewhere to crash. Why wouldn't he? He'd done the same with just about everyone else he'd ever known, bitten the hand of anyone who'd ever fed or loved him. And of course if Sonja had chosen to help him, she'd have known better than to tell her mum about it.

But – and she strongly approved of her son-in-law, in this one regard at least – Simon wouldn't let Sonja have anything to do with Ned now, she was certain of that. Simon may have ingested the odd substance, but he didn't want a deadbeat druggie hanging round his wife and kids.

Returning from the en-suite, Colleen could tell Billy was about to ask another tricky question, so she quickly asked if she should dress up Grandad so they could play a game of that old favourite, *Bed Monster!*

'*Yaayyyyyyyyyyyyyyyyyy!*' came the reply, delirious and predictable.

Andrew greeted this suggestion with a weary smile. Basically, the kids went off to hide – they could go anywhere they liked, but according to tradition they just always hid under the covers in their own beds – while Grandad dressed up as some sort of grotesque character who would come and track them down. There wasn't much more to it than that, really; it was all about the build-up, and the reveal of the latest monster outfit.

Delightedly terrified already, the pair ran off squealing, leaving Colleen and Andrew to improvise a truly awful get-up for him: the hen-shaped oven glove on his head, wire coat-hangers for earrings (a touch dangerous, perhaps, but oddly effective), a pair of safety goggles over his eyes that she'd found in the boiler cupboard, a dollop of her hand cream rubbed roughly over his face, with a generous smear of her magenta lipstick à la Robert Smith, an inside-out floral dressing gown, and marigold gloves on the ends of his feet.

Though she said it herself, he looked absolutely *hideous*. 'Go get 'em,' she whispered, giving him a peck on his smeary cheek.

To keep the twins' anticipation going, Andrew would periodically utter throaty gurgling noises of a terrifying zomboid timbre, and Colleen would give little horrified *oohs* and *ahhs* at the monstrous spectacle that was emerging before her eyes. All these sound effects were stagey enough to carry to the little ones' room, of course, from where both grandparents were gratified to hear more squeals of delighted terror.

'Und now . . . !' said Andrew, emerging from his bedroom. 'I come to find und eat YOU!' His zombie accent had turned a little Nazi, she noticed.

'What's up? I smell a device! My dear fellow, you look absolutely a picture!'

Andrew stopped, and turned. There in the kitchen was Wolf, leaning against a kitchen surface and enjoying a cup of coffee with Sonja.

'Goodness gracious me, these couples from London, they get up to all sorts in the privacy of their holiday cottages!' Wolf seemed highly amused. 'Great news, Andrew – Tony says he can make it this evening to come and look at the car. Also: I'm driving up to the shops. I wondered if you needed any provisions?' He glanced around the kitchen, browsed the crossword, took in the table laden still with breakfast things. 'Some builder's tea maybe? PG perhaps? Or are you Yorkshire people?'

'Do you know, Wolf, it's *so* funny you should say that,' said Sonja. 'Mum and Dad have been arguing about which is better for years!'

Wolf feigned shock. 'Not arguing too violently, I trust? I hope you haven't come to blows?'

'Oh, no, no. Just a . . . friendly disagreement.'

'I see,' said Wolf, adding with a twinkle: 'One might say . . . a storm in a teacup.' His shoulders heaved up and down with quiet merriment.

Everyone laughed. It was actually hard not to. Not so much at the joke, but at the pleasure this tall, odd, kindly sex-slave was giving himself.

'Ach, yes. Mrs Wolf and I have those from time to time,' he continued wisely. 'But of course there are only two ways in any household. Are there not, Andrew?'

'Er, what are they?' said Andrew, who was still poised in the corridor, and probably starting to feel a little bit self-conscious. It was the coat-hanger earrings, no doubt.

'Why – her way and the wrong way, of course!' he snorted delightedly. 'But my dear man, don't let me keep you. I fancy you have . . . little people to attend upon?'

'I do indeed, Wolf, thank you.' He certainly did. The costume was designed to function only on a very short-term, high-impact, single-use basis. Bits of it were falling off already.

'Well, I'll be leaving in about an hour and a half. Give me a knock if you need anything – or if you just fancy a drive. It's always nice to have a bit of company on the road!'

'Will do, sir!' trilled Andrew. Colleen stared at her husband. *Sir?*

'Right you are – must get on!' said Wolf, rising suddenly. 'I have many hours in the saddle before I can take my rest,' he said with mock-epic fortitude. 'And if I don't tick off the errands on my list, Mrs Wolf will have my garters for guts!'

'Don't you mean guts for garters?' said Andrew, unable to resist.

'That's easy for you to say!' he replied at once, as if anticipating the question. 'Ach, you don't know Mrs Wolf. If I don't get my jobs done, she is apt to beat me to within an inch of my life!'

Everyone laughed. Sonja and Colleen shared a look, and were quickly in discreet hysterics. Andrew laughed too, but it sounded like a forced, conflicted sort of laugh that he was glad to turn into a blood-curling zombie howl. He set off with a last jangly swish of his coat-hanger earrings, fee-fie-foing along the corridor to the little ones' room. Their little hearts would be thrumming with horrified anticipation by now.

'I must keep him away from Mrs Wolf in that outfit,' Wolf confided to the two women in his wake. 'He could turn anyone's head looking like that.'

'Oh, I know what you mean!' said Colleen, 'He's quite the dish, isn't he?'

'Oh yes,' agreed Wolf enthusiastically. 'I'll wager tonight might be someone's *lucky night*! Toodle-pip!'

'Bye!' called Colleen, noticing suddenly that she had stopped smiling.

II. NEAR-MISS

After Andrew got rid of his costume, and was then induced to take part in another madcap half hour of donkey-pirate-chase up on the meadow, itself supplemented with a lightning round of the newly coined egg-monkey game [a game that resisted easy explanation, except for the inevitable Grandad-chasing element], Wolf emerged, Cavalry-like, to see if Andrew and the children would like to take Jack for a walk in the woods. [Andrew, who believed that there was a secret connection to uncover between any pair of words that were anagrams of each other, wondered about *Cavalry* and *Calvary*. [Being back with the little ones, meanwhile, had helped him understand at last the link between *sausage* and *assuage*.]]

Sonja stayed behind with Colleen, while Wolf and Jack led Andrew and the twins carefully over the road and into the forest. Once safely across, they ran on ahead, looking for fallen trunks to clamber on and sticks that would make decent wands.

'You're really great with those children, you know, old boy,' said Wolf. 'They have such fun with you.'

'Oh, thank you! It's just nice to spend time with them.'

'My father wasn't like that at all. He was a difficult man. Austere.'

'Austere how? Cold-showers-and-early-morning-runs austere?' said Andrew, pleased to spot an extended phrasal modifier in the wild, even if was his own.

'Oh, not quite like that. More sort of, lock-you-in-a-stifling-cupboard-with-a-rabid-dog-and-no-food-and-water-for-a-day austere,' said Wolf, with impressive syntactic parallelism. 'Jack! Here, boy! Come!' He strode off to see to the dog, which was now barking at a phantom rabbit in a patch of bramble, leaving Andrew grateful that he was not expected to come up with an appropriate response to this intimacy.

Looking at Wolf striding around with the kids and the dog, helping them to find sticks shaped like the first letters of their names and pointing out interesting fauna, Andrew reflected that he seemed in very good spirits – and looked remarkably intact – for a man recently seen lying on the floor while his furious wife beats him. In fact, he looked so chipper, so much larger than life, that Andrew – never a strong believer in reality at the best of times – quickly began to wonder if he'd dreamed up the whole scene.

When they came together again, it was clear that the subject of his father was now closed. Wolf whistled a sort of wolf-whistle.

'But what a shame they couldn't all be here?' said Wolf.

'All?'

'You know – Ned, is it?'

Andrew felt suddenly winded and nauseous.

'Ned?'

'Yes! Isn't that Sonja's husband's name? Your son . . . in-law?'

'No! Sonja's husband – that's Simon.'

'Oh, I do beg your parsnip, old man.'

Andrew looked at his Fitbit. He was already over 5300 for the day. It was a shock to hear his son's name, the name he dared not even say out loud to his wife, from the mouth of this eccentric character. Wolf must have heard the kids say it. Andrew had been secretly pleased to hear that Billy and Ginny remembered Ned too, if not exactly in person then at least as an essential piece of their family jigsaw. Ned who was not dead, but who was so conspicuously absent he might as well have been.

It wasn't easy to find a moment to discuss it freely, but Sonja had hinted that she still heard from him, though hadn't seen him. He doubted if she gave him money, over the years he'd had so much of hers already – some volunteered, much stolen. Very much not for the first time, Andrew wondered if he could entrust his daughter with the knowledge of his own clandestine payments. But was it fair to implicate her in his deception?

One thing Andrew was sure of: Simon wouldn't have Ned in the house. Simon, who liked to play the part of a debonair hedonist, but would throw up his whole sophisticated defence system at the merest hint of a brush with real life. He knew it was a hopeless Dad thing to say, of course, but: *what on earth did she ever see in him?* He had money, of course, but he barked and brayed and he had mean little eyes. The more he stayed away, frankly, the better for Sonja. And the twins.

Jack was delighted to be out in the woods with so many new friends. He bounced around the kids excitedly, but he seemed careful not to knock them and he didn't bark once.

'*Get away from there, children! Jack – you know better!*' Wolf's voice was suddenly stern, almost guttural. [Good word, *guttural.*] While Andrew and Wolf had been strolling along a central path of the woods, he saw now that Billy and Ginny had wandered off down a little overhung alley that led into a little copse of shrubby, bushy things [he was not a horticultural man], each of which contained a little enclosed hollow area where a couple of children could have fun hiding from a dog.

The children had been running in and out of these, but had now stopped before what appeared at first glance to be a little den. There were piles of sticks, artfully arranged according to some pattern he couldn't as yet fathom, and freshly cut flowers. A child's windmill, some teddies, a doll. Billy had picked up a bright little orange ball and was throwing it up for Ginny to catch. Jack, meanwhile, was sniffing piteously at a raised earthed-up area, atop which – Andrew saw now with horror – a rudimentary wooden cross had been affixed. There was no time to look closely, but it appeared to have some numbers carved into it.

'Oh God. Quickly, children! This way!'

He looked at Wolf's face, and saw for a moment an expression of tremendously weary pain. Ushering the children back onto the main path, he crouched down to their eye level.

'Now what do you two both say to . . . ?' He stopped. 'What do you both say?'

The little ones looked at their feet. It pained Andrew to see how easily he could bully them into a display of contrition they didn't deserve and could not hope to understand.

'Ach, no! No! You've done nothing, children!'

For Wolf, it seemed, the moment was over as suddenly as it had arrived. He became even more playful and energetic on the way back, challenging the kids to jump a small stream, schooling them in the way of Poohsticks and showing them how to make a range of [largely indistinguishable] bird calls with cupped palms.

He even, under careful supervision, let Billy and then Ginny take turns holding Jack's leash. And of course, they loved it. The grave moment had been quite forgotten.

'If only it was so easy to hold life on a lead, no?' said Wolf, with a sniffle. There was a large drip of something forming at the tip of his nose; Andrew had a sudden urge to reach out and wipe it.

'That's . . . a very, uh, philosophical observation, if I may say so,' said Andrew. He was aware of his reply as a sort of holding response, until he could figure out where the conversation was heading and how he would negotiate it if things got more personal. He was going to add 'Wolf', but he still couldn't do it.

'Oh, you know. The things we can't control are the ones that threaten to hurt us the most. *Whoooaa, children!'*

A pickup truck was hurtling past them, loud and violent. Wolf stepped in nimbly to restrain the children at the roadside, but they screamed in fright. Jack barked angrily after the speeding driver.

'Bloody hell,' Andrew said, a couple of steps behind. 'Thank you, Wolf.'

'Oh, don't be silly,' he said. 'You were here too. You would have caught them in time.' Wolf bent down to the young boy, who was still holding Jack. 'I better take the lead back off you now, Master Billy,' he said. 'We don't want the ladies thinking I've been leading you astray.'

'Yes,' said Andrew, unconvinced. His heart was pounding; he hadn't been thinking about the road at all. He had been ruminating on Wolf's words about leashes and control, thinking again about Ned as a child.

'Oh, yes,' said Wolf, affectionately tousling first Billy's hair then Ginny's. 'You wouldn't let anything happen to your adorable twins.'

'No,' said Andrew, trying to sound reassured. 'Of course not.'

'Not on your watch.'

By the time they got back to the house, Sonja was already starting to load her Qashqi [or CashCard, as he liked to call it]. There was a frostiness in the air, and Colleen was nowhere to be seen.

III. NO HUGS, NO REGRETS

As Sonja's snazzy white car scrunched over the gravel and turned sharply out onto the road with a final toot of the horn, some muffled shouts from the kids and a last wave from the driver's window, Colleen – watching quietly from her bedroom – felt suddenly overpowered by sadness.

Her phone dinged. Gerry had texted again, and she had two missed calls from another client, Baz.

Baz was a senior partner with a private equity fund. He was a Master of his Universe, a man who commanded great respect and fear in his industry. If Baz decided to back your business, Colleen understood, your business would smash it – so long as you were prepared to do exactly what Baz told you. What this meant in practice was that you would probably have to sack half your team, including all the people you got the business off the ground with, no matter that you owed it all to them and they were your best mates (or even your spouse, in one case that Baz always liked to crow about).

'This is business,' he liked to say, with a stab of his vaping stick thing. 'No cuddles, no regrets.'

The funny thing about Baz, though, was that beneath this harsh abrasive exterior, and unknown to even his closest friends and family, he had – over the last two or three years – become an anxious, terrified wreck.

This man who had grown a global firm and made keynote speeches at high-profile conferences attended by world leaders was now filled with acute sociophobic dread ahead of even the most modest meet-up in a pub or restaurant. He lay awake every night, sweating with panic. His anxiety floated free over his world, making him phobic about everything from tunnels to wasps to gas canisters and aerosols, which he was convinced were always about to explode.

Baz. *Jesus.* She would have to call him. It was the very last thing she wanted to do after the morning she'd had, but she would have to call him.

She stabbed at his name with her index finger, then heaved a big out-breath when she saw the call go straight to message. *Reprieved.* For the moment at least.

The moment the kids were out of sight and over the road, a pointed silence had kicked in between mother and daughter.

'Do you want a coffee?' said Sonja.

'Yes, please, love. One sugar.'

'Since when do you have sugar?'

'I'm on holiday, aren't I? Living *la vida loca*, me.'

'You certainly both seem very abstemious for a couple on holiday,' said Sonja, pretending to study the crossword.

'Oh, you know, it's nice to have a bit of a detox from time to time. I'm enjoying it actually. Makes you feel sort of . . . sharper.'

Sonja put the paper down. 'I saw the email, Mum.'

Colleen's heart gave a single, alarming jolt. Reflexively, she touched her hair, scratching at an imaginary itch somewhere round the back of her head.

'What email?' They both knew she was stalling for time. But there was just too much time in the world for her to be able to stall it all.

'*You know.* The one from Paul and Paul.'

Paul and Paul – known, when it was necessary to distinguish them, as Tall-Paul and Pond-Paul – were among their oldest friends. Colleen had met Tall-Paul at drama school; he was the only one of her friends from that time that Andrew had ever really got on with. (The evenings with Andrew and Gerry, though there had been a few down the years, were always tense affairs, especially as the night wore on and people said stuff.)

Tall-Paul – who was actually about five foot eight – had a natural gift for making money, and quickly saw there wasn't much of that in acting, unless you were really lucky or super-beautiful. And he wasn't really either of those, bless him, even if he was incredible with accents and impersonations. So Tall-Paul went into recruitment instead, then property, and now ran an exclusive little estate agency in a fancier neck of north London than hers and Andrew's. (Tall-Paul characterised Colleen's area as FSS or 'family-suburban strivers'; his patch, he said, was more MAA or 'mature affluent achievers'.) It was through this work that he'd met Pond-Paul, so called because he designed saunas and landscaped gardens for the sort of people who bought and sold Tall-Paul's properties. The two Pauls were one of the first couples in the UK to get a civil partnership.

Proper couple friends were very hard to come by. Colleen had a theory that there was only one true couple friendship in the world for any couple. By a true couple friendship, she meant a foursome that wasn't based on A's friendship with former colleague C, say, with B and D forced to smile politely and make exhausted small talk from the sidelines. Or one where A and B absolutely *love* C, whom they know from uni, but only barely tolerate D, whom C has decided to marry for some reason that neither A or B (or even, they suspect, C) can fathom.

No. The friendship Colleen and Andrew enjoyed with the two Pauls was a proper . . . *four-mance*. (That wasn't the word; she would leave it to Andrew to think one up.) They got on in any combination, whether there were two, three or four of them. They shared a love of silly games, eighties music and fine food. They liked nothing more than to try out a new local French or Italian or Indian, and they all loved a long, lazy Sunday roast in the pub.

Whisper it, but both Pauls also happened to be partial to a drop or two, which was why their email was so unfair. In fact they probably wrote it pissed, come to think of it.

'How do you know about that?'

She was alert now, defensive. She loved her daughter, but for as long as she could remember, they had always had a way of rubbing each other up the wrong way. Pushing buttons, pressing on bruises. Sonja had started it last night by mentioning . . . And now all Colleen's overnight pledges to herself about not losing her temper, about getting past the crap and having a proper heart-to-heart about Simon and the kids, were out the window.

'How do you know about any email?' she said again. She still held a teeny, tiny candle for the idea that Sonja was referring to some other email.

'They sent it to me too, Mum. Must have bcc-ed it.'

'What email? What did it say?'

'Mum. Come on. The one that begins with the story about you in Cafe Amalfi . . .'

Oh, crap.

'. . . and ends with them begging you both to seek help.'

'Yeah, right. It's them that needs help. The whole thing's just a massive projection.'

99

'Mum.'

'Did you see what time they sent it? Four o'clock in the fucking morning! They must have been off their faces.'

They looked at each other, aghast. Colleen couldn't remember ever having sworn in front of her daughter before.

Sonja shot Colleen yet another *do-we-really-have-do-this* type look, while Colleen sat steaming in shame. She felt like the subject of an intervention on Jeremy Kyle. One of those characters who is in denial about their denial, and they're the only ones who can't see it.

She felt like the elephant in the room.

Except of course she had nothing to deny. She suddenly felt a pang of sympathy for all those people in the world who are accused by self-righteous caring types of being in denial, *but actually aren't*. But how could you prove you weren't in denial if everyone else decided that you were? All you could do was deny the denial – but that, of course, would just play right into their hands.

She said, 'Actually, I don't think Tall-Paul had anything to do with it.'

'What?'

'It's Pond-Paul. He's had a problem for years. Tried to keep it quiet. I've had long chats with Tall-Paul about it many a time.'

'Mum.'

'It's made him quite unstable, Tall-Paul reckons. He's really torn up about it, as you can imagine.'

Sonja made no reply, just looked pointedly at her mum yet again.

'I haven't shown Tall-Paul the email because he probably doesn't know about it and I don't want to upset him further.'

More looking from Sonja. Of the pointed variety.

'On the other hand, it *is* a sort of plea for help. I think he's sort of *reaching out* to us, in a twisted sort of way.'

Then Sonja said the thing that effectively brought an end to her little visit.

'Well, Mum,' she said. 'If anyone knows the best way to deal with addicts . . .'

She was halfway out the door as she said it, off to pack her bags and gather up the last of the kids' bits.

Now, with her daughter and her daughter's kids gone, Colleen was empty. Andrew was out pacing the meadow to get his steps up or chatting with Wolf about the car yet again – *oh, fix it already, for the love of God!* Baz called, and she made herself answer. He was unusually upbeat, positively triumphant.

'I had the board meet this morning and I was shitting myself, I don't mind telling you,' he said. 'So I did exactly what you said, babe.'

'Oh. What was that?' She was sitting on the backdoor step. As she'd hoped, the little black cat was back again. With another newborn cry of greeting, it had snaked through a gap in the bottom of the fence and come trotting over on padded feet to within a yard of her.

'You know – look for a way to distract myself, let off some steam.'

'Oh, right, yes. So what did you do?' She held out her hand. The cat toyed with the idea of approaching her. Two steps forward, one little jump back; the familiar dance. Its front two feet were white socks, she saw, and there was a little streak of fluffy white underneath too.

'So I've gone to the gym first thing, and I've kicked seven lumps of shit out of my sparring partner. Then, just before the meet, I've gone to the loo and I've banged one right out. *Incoming!* Just like you said.'

'Oh? Well. I'm not sure I . . .'

'Then I've mopped myself up, obviously, and I've gone in that boardroom . . . *and I've absolutely smashed it.* I've gone in there, forgotten all the nerves, kicked the shit out of every-one. And all thanks to you, Colleen. You are an absolute fecking diamond.'

'Well, I mean . . . I'm just so glad it worked out.'

'I hope you've got some availability, love, because I'm going to be recommending you to the rest of my senior management team. They're fucking fruitcakes, the lot of them. And they're all first-class wankers already!' Colleen held the phone away from her ear as Baz guffawed violently. The cat jumped, and she watched with a helpless pang as it shot off, leaping back over the fence in a single fluid movement.

'That's . . . really great to hear! Thanks, Baz!'

'Think nothing of it, babe. You're a fucking lifesaver.'

Duty done, Colleen re-read the Pauls' email. She called and called, but the cat did not re-appear. Then she slipped into the utility room, slipped a bottle of Absolut vodka out from its hiding-place and took a swift, deep swig.

And it was still only Tuesday.

IV. DRIFTING OUT OF THE GAME

As Andrew lapped the meadow once more, his mind wandered to the evening ahead of them. Would there, could there be sex? Not that it mattered, not that he was counting.

The children had departed in a blizzard of hugs and heartfelt goodbyes that still rang around his delighted ears. They liked him, they really did, and their adorable waves and smiles were only slightly eclipsed by the strange absence of Colleen. No doubt she and Sonja had had words, perhaps about Simon, but probably about Ned. A shame to take it out on the grandkids, but there it was.

He should never have left them on their own. They *always* ended up having words. Perhaps he had allowed his cautious but growing sense of optimism about the week [and there was possible sex tonight, never forget [not that it mattered, not that he was counting]] to get the better of him. He and Colleen were really trying; his mistake had been to assume that Sonja and Colleen would be trying as hard too.

As he walked he kicked out at an old Jack-bitten football. It was a yellow one bearing the insignia of the last World Cup, quite a nice ball once. Ned had been a good footballer in his day, far better than his dad by the end. Andrew had been a showy inside-right as a youngster, a nippy forward with a couple of tricks but not much bottle, quickly found out by any player with a bit of steel to them. Ned, on the other hand, had been a proper attacking midfielder, a brave box-to-box playmaker who made strong driving runs forward into dangerous positions. He had really very good ball control as he ran, and in a crunching 50:50 he was always the one who came away with it.

Had he himself been any good as a dad? Sonja had turned out well, even if she couldn't get on with her mum, and her kids were a joy. He and his daughter had always had an understanding, always had a way of getting on, to the exclusion of the others at times, perhaps. With Ned, he felt he had tried hard, tried to do all the obvious right things – took him to football, got him involved in drama, a running club, even judo at one point. But nothing seemed to stick somehow, just as in their conversations he and Ned never seemed to progress beyond a certain level of connection. He loved his son very much, he ached at times for his presence, and a worry for his welfare ticked away endlessly in the back of his mind. But he wasn't sure that he had ever really known him.

Back in the day, assuming the position of Dad on the touchline, Andrew would watch as Ned ran past the opposition and played the ball into intelligent space, thoughtlessly putting his body on the line, timing tackles and blocks that turned defence into attack. He was quietly impressive, and he drew the eye. You looked to him for more . . . but every time, as the clock ticked on, Ned had a way of drifting out of the game. He played deeper and deeper, he hung back, he quickly and unnecessarily recycled the ball any time it came near him. He tracked back when his team attacked, passed when he could have shot. He seemed to have a knack of being where the action wasn't, and he was frequently guilty of playing opposing attackers on side.

It was as if he wasn't really there. A similar refusal to play the game seemed to happen with his school work, his friendship groups, everything really. Had he been leading a life of quiet desperation all those years? Had he been secretly out of his depth all that time, not waving but drowning? Perhaps if they'd let him get a job, as at one point he'd said he wanted to do, instead of nagging and prodding him all those evenings to do the revision that would enable him to scrape into college? Perhaps if they'd let him stay on at the supermarket, where he at least kept a regular routine and earned a bit of cash?

Perhaps if Andrew had been a different kind of dad.

In the event, it probably didn't matter whether he stayed on at the store or got a different job or went to college, because that was the summer he met Leah. None of those other choices mattered, unless they could have prevented that. Overnight, everything about Ned changed: his clothes, his taste in music, his attitude to his family, his attitude to other people's possessions [and especially their money], even his hygiene levels [initially at least]. Certainly he and Leah loved each other, albeit in some doomed, narcotic way; certainly there was a lot of sex, often embarrassingly blatant sex. Was it wrong to blame Leah as much as Colleen did? Perhaps the transformation that took place over the next eighteen months would have happened anyway. But it was certainly in Leah's suffocating company and under her dubious influence that Ned effected the transition from a teenage dopehead slacker to a full-blown dropout who was ready to ingest or inject anything that came his way.

A sudden unexpected breeze caused Andrew to shiver. He was over 8500 on his steps now, and would soon be in what he liked to call the SafeZone – the last 750 steps, which you could be pretty confident of knocking off just pottering about the house in the course of your domestic evening. [On the list tonight: bins, recycling, see Wolf about car again, look up drive for tomorrow.] [Did sex count as steps, by the way? He hadn't had much cause to confirm this one way or the other recently.] [There might be some tonight actually, not that it mattered, not that he was counting.]

He heard a car draw up and a door slam and then Jack barking before he saw him. Now Wolf came into view, triumphantly waving a packet of Yorkshire tea and a packet of PG Tips. 'I didn't want to be the cause of any marital disruptions!' he shouted. 'So I got you one of each.'

He was a sweet man. An odd sexual masochist perhaps, but a sweet man. It was weird that Wolf had mentioned Ned's name earlier. But it moved him too somehow.

Wolf clicked the meadow gate open and strode over to meet Andrew, who was approaching from the other end. Wolf handed over the packets of tea with a grand flourish.

'Don't forget this, dear boy!' he called. He handed Andrew his iPhone, which – thinking he might actually jog a few steps – he had left on the gatepost as he entered the field.

'Oh God, thanks, Wolf. What would we do without you?'

'Ach, I'm sure you'd manage.'

'Any luck with Tony? I don't mean to hassle or anything.'

'Not hassling at all, my dear sir! Still waiting to hear, alas. I've left a couple of messages.'

It would be another evening in the cottage tonight then.

'We're thinking of getting an Indian delivered,' said Andrew. 'Anyone you'd recommend?'

'The Golden Raj, every time!' Wolf beamed. 'I should get a commission for all the times I've recommended them.'

'Right. Great. Deal! I remember the leaflet from your very welcoming . . . welcome pack.'

'And don't forget you've got that wine to wash it down with!'

'Oh, yes,' said Andrew with a faint pang. At this rate they would have to tip the red down the sink just to prove to Wolf that they'd drunk it. That might not be such a bad idea, in point of fact, though the thought of such wastefulness panicked him.

'Unless of course there is another tipple you prefer?'

'Ooh, I don't think so.'

'A spot of vodka perhaps? I can always drop some round.'

'Oh, no. But that's very kind. You've done far too much already.'

'Think nothing of it, old boy. It's an Absolut pleasure. Or gin? Or Scotch? We've even got some Jack Daniels, I believe. But only some of those little ones, you know?'

Andrew shuffled a little where he stood.

'You're very kind. But actually, we're having a bit of a detox this week.'

'Quite right. Well, far be it from me to tempt you from the ways of righteousness.'

'Thanks again, Wolf. For everything.' He was aware of having used the name for the first time. He looked for a reaction, but there was none.

'Please, not another word. Your twins are lucky to have you, I'm sure.'

'My twins?'

'Do forgive me! Your daughter's twins, I mean.'

'Oh! Well, we're the lucky ones.'

'They're so young and innocent, it's adorable.'

'They certainly are.'

'It's funny to think though that one day they'll be grown up and it'll be a quite different kettle of fish, won't it?' mused Wolf, looking off sagely into the distance. 'Almost impossible to imagine really: boyfriends, girlfriends, cars, music. Drinking, drugs, rock and roll! Keeping you up all hours, asking for money . . .'

Andrew was not a man to make eye contact unless eye contact was absolutely necessary, which was pretty much never, in his book. But now he looked Wolf square between the eyes. For a moment. Wolf beamed blithely back.

'Anyway, let me go and give Tony another call,' he said. 'Wouldn't it be great if we could get this car thing sorted out tonight?'

He left Andrew standing there, with his phone and his teabags.

V. BETWEEN TWO MINDS

Andrew took one look at Colleen's face and knew something was wrong. She swept past him in a flurry of face-mask and bathrobe and citrus scent, heading for yet another bath, perhaps the fourth or fifth of her stay. Soon enough, he could hear the low roar of the taps and scent the oil-infused steam that portended another ominous soak.

Andrew knew all about Colleen and baths. A single bath could be a sign of letting off steam after a hard day or week, a prelude to going out and letting her hair down, or even a sign that she was contemplating the making of love. [Something, he remembered again, that had been mooted as a possible thing that might possibly happen this evening. Possibly.] [Not that it mattered in the scheme of things, not that he was counting.] But several baths in a period of a few short days tended to be a symptom of unease. At times when

107

they hadn't been getting on, or when Sonja first started getting serious about Simon, or of course during the dark time of Ned's last days at home, Colleen seemed always to be retreating to the bath as a refuge, an escape from the realities of what was happening. The door would be locked shut with a forbidding metallic click, and from long experience Andrew knew better than to try and break the seal of Colleen's watery refuge. To burst her *bath bubble*, if you will. [Christ, even now! It was an affliction.]

So, as a rule of thumb: one bath good; multiple baths bad. With the bathroom door locked, Andrew decided that now was, in the scheme of things, perhaps as good a time as any to nip out into the garden and check the peg bag. All was well, as he quickly discovered: there were his babies, all tucked up safely in their calico bed. He would have no need of them this week, of course, but it was good to know they were there. Indeed, the very fact of them being there – and this sort of thing was hard to explain to others sometimes, he wasn't quite sure why – meant that they wouldn't be needed. So why have something that you don't intend to use? Well, why have nuclear warheads? It was simple really. Just a small matter of game theory and deterrence logic.

He looked at the crossword. He noted that another clue had been filled in.

11 down (3, 2, 6): Vagrant consumed by angry goat turns up trumps

The answer, according to the addition made in a black felt tip pen whose ink was distressingly runny, was 'Bum in butter'. It was elegant enough as a clue, and quite easy really, now he looked at it. But subject-wise, there was a sort of callousness to the clue that he wasn't sure he approved of. He similarly disliked clues that appeared to be flippant about serious real-life issues, such as 'Middle-East solution' [typically just a reference to the middle two letters of east] or 'an end to the Backstop' [just a lazy way of extracting the 'p' of an answer].

Colleen would say, of course, that it was a measure of his political complacency and moral cowardice that the only issues he could get mildly worked up about related to the language of crossword clues. And even then, these were just things to tut over. [He called to mind that Peter Cook and Dudley Moore sketch in which Sir Arthur Grieb-Striebling claims to have been 'completely against' the Second World War. 'Well, I think we all were,' counters Moore. 'Ah, yes,' says Sir Arthur Grieb-Striebling. 'But *I* wrote *a letter.*']

He looked at the two packets of tea on the kitchen table. Colleen had remarked earlier that day that it was a weird coincidence that Wolf had come up with the two brands they always squabbled over. [Friendly squabbles, of course.] Was it coincidence, however, that Wolf had alluded to Jack Daniels miniatures? Was it just him, or was this not a tad uncanny? Wolf had also talked about having to stay up all night sorting out money for your kids, which seemed uncomfortably close to home too. But no. These things always start to seem weird when you go looking for them; it was one of those cognitive bias thingies. The grandkids had mentioned Ned, that was how he knew his name. And even if Wolf had seen the bottles, it was obvious that . . .

Oh, stop it. He couldn't possibly have seen the bottles. He was nosy for sure, and perhaps a bit of a control freak, but it was impossible for him to know about that. And that grave in the woods. What was that? His face. The poor man.

By the time the takeaway was delivered there was a distinct tension in the air. Andrew had busied himself with whatever chores he could find: washing and drying up a few dishes, wiping down surfaces that didn't really need wiping, and remembering to follow Wolf's instruction to keep an eye on the sink in the utility room, which had to his regret been fitted not quite straight, with the result that if left unchecked water could roll off and down on to the wooden boxing that covered the pipework below.

When Colleen finally emerged from her bath, she seemed far from relaxed. His inner marital barometer sensed a build-up of pressure in the cottage's emotional weather that was only likely to blow one way.

Colleen stood in the doorway in her dressing gown. Her skin glowed and her hair was up. He thought she looked marvellous. Also a little enraged.

'Why did you let her see it?'

'Who?'

'Sonja.'

'See what?'

'Oh, *stop*. The fucking email.'

So that was it.

'I didn't show it to her. They sent it.'

'I don't believe you. Paul would never do that.'

'Have you asked him?'

'I don't need to.'

'Not the strongest argument.'

'Oh, stop it.' There was an edge to her voice he didn't want to recognise.

'They all want us to stop. They're only trying to help.'

'So you *did* send it to her.'

He was seized by a reckless impulse for honesty. 'Yes! I thought we'd have a better chance of getting through this if we let other people in a little. Got their support.'

She stood up. For a moment she looked about as if trying to find something to throw. She was beside herself with rage.

'Christ, you make me sick! What gives you the right to parade my life to the world? Without even telling *me*?'

She was making a more compelling argument now, and a more compelling answer was called for.

'Colleen,' he said. 'I love you.' *Jesus*, he hadn't known he was going to say that. He did love her, God knows he did, but that was shouting the odds and he was only just getting going. If he started his case there, where could he go next?

'Oh, spare me.'

'I do! And I just want us to get through this.'

'You and Sonja have been having a great time, haven't you, talking about me behind my back.'

'Well, hang on. The email doesn't exactly do me any favours either,' he countered, but she wasn't listening.

'Father and daughter. Loving it all up. Having a high old time, bitching about stupid old pisshead Mum. Aren't Mum's problems funny? How did she get so fucked up? Isn't she . . . *a case?*'

[*Loving it all up*. At first Andrew thought Colleen was making some sort of sinister suggestion. And it was true that she had always resented the bond he shared with Sonja. But then he realised that she was simply conflating 'loving it' and 'lapping it up'. High emotion often triggers such dysfluencies, as he was ashamed to be noting at such a time.]

'I love you, Colleen. I want us to get through this.'

'If you wanted us to get through this, why are you talking to everyone but me about it?'

Because you always react like this, he wanted to say.

'Because you always . . .' He stopped. 'Sometimes when we try to help each other . . . we somehow end up our own worst enemies.' He thought this sounded rather good.

'Oh, *fuck off*.' Oh.

'Can't we get past this?'

'Get past it? Put it in a magic box and forget all about it?'

Though the anger was still raw, he sensed that the threat of things being thrown was subsiding.

111

Colleen sat down. 'I just can't do this any more!' she cried. 'I can't just pretend.'

Side by side, their mobiles beeped. Andrew itched to check his, or at least to move it out of view; he sensed Colleen was just as anxious to get to hers.

'Who's texting you?' he said.

'No one,' she said. 'Probably Sonja. Checking in on me again.'

'Let me get your phone for you.'

'*No!*' she said, forcefully. She walked across to the chargers, picked up her phone and stalked out of the room. Andrew stood on in the living room, wondering if his message was from Ned but not daring to check. He heard the back door open. Was Colleen smoking again? He had already decided not to make a thing about this. He heard a dog's bark and some whistling from Wolf's back garden.

When Colleen came back into the living room, she was carrying some little things.

'*Here*,' she spat, and flung a handful at him across the room. 'If you're so keen to move on and fix things, what have you bought these for?'

Andrew bent over and started picking up his miniatures.

'You wouldn't understand,' he said helplessly. 'They're a deterrent. They're not there to be drunk.'

He sounded ridiculous, even to himself.

'It's game theory,' he added lamely.

'Well, my *theory* is that this is all a big game to you,' said Colleen.

'I was never going to drink any of them . . .' he began hopelessly. 'Whereas you . . .'

He heard a small click. Colleen had cracked one and was now necking it with abandon. She seemed not to have noticed that her robe had fallen open.

'"Does thou think because thou art virtuous",' she quoted, '"there shall be no more cakes and ale?"'

He stood atop a precipice. The chasm yawned. The wind howled. But then he was not standing, he was prone, and the wind was his cushion as he fell through the vortex of bad faith that swirled between his two minds. The fall was . . . delicious.

'Chin chin,' he said, opening his first.

WEDNESDAY

*What can we say? Paul and I love you both, you know we
do. But over the last few months, you have turned into one
of those terrifying booze couples. The ones you see bitterly
arguing about whose turn it is to drive because it's
11.30am and you're both half-cut already. Or who spend
evenings at parties sitting in opposite corners, getting
completely legless and bitching to whoever will listen about
the other one.*

Please – isn't it time to ask for some help?

I. CASUALTIES OF WAR

On Wednesday, at the ungodly hour of 10.45am, there was
the sound of thin heavy wheels on gravel, accompanied by
cheerful whistling and some light but infuriating barking.

'Hello, hello!' called Wolf, rapping briskly and calling out
with infernal bonhomie. 'Is anyone at home? Are the lady
and gentleman of the house decent?'

Wolf had wheeled Mrs Wolf – correction, Hildy – over to
the cottage back door. He had, he said, 'a cunning plan'.
Tony the mechanic had yet to reply. So he and Andrew would
go over to Tony's themselves, pick him up and bring him
back to look at the car.

In the meantime, Wolf wondered whether Andrew's good
lady wife might like to visit with Mrs Wolf?

'My name is Hildy, Wolf!' scolded Hildy, with a despairing heavenwards look for Colleen's benefit.

Colleen, who was struggling at this moment to stay vertical without vomiting, thought this was a terrible idea.

'What a lovely idea!' she said at once. 'Tell you what, why don't you give us a few minutes to make ourselves decent and we'll come and knock for you.' She flapped at her flimsy dressing gown. 'Would that be OK?'

'Oh! I see!' cackled Wolf with obvious delight. 'Someone's been at the cooking sherry!'

'Oh, it's not that,' said Colleen. 'We just stayed up rather late . . . watching Netflix.' The older couple looked unconvinced. Colleen was seized by a sudden inspiration. She leaned across conspiratorially, hoping she didn't smell a fraction of how bad she felt, and whispered: 'I'm an absolute sucker for *Dexter* . . . You know, the serial killer.'

Hildy looked nonplussed an instant, but then understanding dawned. 'Ooh, yes,' she said. 'The sexy psycho.' She nodded in the direction of Wolf, whose face was still a blank. And then she cackled in a way that Colleen could only describe as, well – and this really wasn't like her – *very vulgar.*

'I can see you two are hitting it off already!' said Wolf, beginning the cumbersome process of swinging the wheelchair around.

Hildy patted Colleen on a thigh. 'You come to me when you're ready, dear,' she said. 'We'll have a laugh. Put these men to rights.'

Andrew was in the shower when she headed back inside. She had only got up because she needed a pee. She poured herself two instant coffees, added sugar and a bit of tepid tap water to each, and necked them fast, one after the other.

The kitchen was littered with empty miniatures. A bottle of Absolut lay vacantly on its side under a chair. The gifted wine bottle, now also bereft of its contents, sat in the sink, awkwardly propped on a couple of foil trays from the Indian takeaway, like a casualty of war.

They had drunk, and they had fought, and they had shagged, though in what order was hard now to determine. It seemed to her vaguely that they had done all of them at once, like in some quantum parallel universe thing.

Drinking and fighting and shagging, that was how they rolled, apparently. The difficult thing to remember was which of the three they had done last, which was unfortunate, because without knowing this it would be hard to know how to behave when Andrew emerged from his shower. Were they currently not speaking? Or post-coitally amorous? Or in mid-confrontation? Perhaps he was feeling as messed up as she was, in which case a truce could be called while they pulled themselves together and tried to get their stories straight.

She got in the shower. It was a big walk-in one, and she'd forgotten Andrew was already in there. He looked round sheepishly.

'Don't mind me,' she said, lathering up with a vigour she forced herself to fake. Andrew stopped whatever he was doing but made a noise, some sort of grunted acknowledgement. A gesture in the direction of language, as he might say. She nodded sympathetically. He sounded like she felt.

'Better get cracking,' she said. 'Wolf's taking you round Tony's in a bit. While I entertain his, uh, lady wife.'

'Oh, God.'

Andrew stepped out of the shower and began applying a towel gingerly to his scalp. As he did so, she couldn't help noticing a long scratch on his temple.

'You've cut yourself,' she said.

He looked at her, not unkindly.

'Oh,' she said. 'Did I . . . ?'

He shook his head. 'I asked for it,' he said. And then he added, 'It was quite a night.'

116

She nodded. 'Quite a night.'

He leant over and kissed her, probably unnecessarily. Andrew could forgive you anything if you let him have sex every now and then. And besides if she *had* hit him – with what, by the way? A glass, a hand, an onion bhaji? – she had no doubt been sorely provoked. It stood to reason.

'Andrew,' she said.

'Yes, love?'

'If we've got such a problem, how come we both hold down demanding, well-paid jobs?'

'They're called *functional* alcoholics for a reason, love.'

'Oh, *pshaw.*' It was no secret that she liked a drink. Or that he did. Or that when they did indulge, they both liked to let their hair down. Or that their version of letting hair down was a bit livelier than other people's. But she was scrupulous about when she did drink, and when she didn't. She never drank the day before a client session, for example; indeed, she made a point never to book any appointments on a Monday or Tuesday (too close to Sunday, i.e. the weekend). Or Thursdays or Fridays, if at all possible.

Anyway, she had no energy to dwell on what she felt about stuff right now – did she hate Andrew? Should she go and work for Gerry? What was the point of anything? and all the rest. The job at hand was just to pull herself together enough to get through the hour with Mrs Wolf. Correction, *Hildy.* She would need coffee, clothes, make-up, more coffee.

Andrew, bless him, who she could hear was already clearing up the worst of the kitchen, came back in with another coffee, plus two large glasses of fizzy water, two orange juices and two aspirin each. After that, they would need another glass of water, this time with effervescent vitamin B in it, some more coffee, and something fried – a sausage sandwich perhaps, or bacon and eggs. There was a well-rehearsed process with these things, and one of them always remembered it eventually.

She smiled ruefully as she tried to find the energy to begin towelling herself. Sometimes Andrew knew just what she needed. They were never more a team than at times of great crisis like this.

II. CUTTING BOTH WAYS

Back in the cottage, with Colleen having set off uncertainly across the gravel to her appointment, Andrew did his best to attend to his own hangover.

They had drunk a fair bit the night before. That was fair to say. He had meant to hold firm and stay sober all week, he really had. But he couldn't do it alone, he didn't want to do it alone.

He made himself a double fried egg, sprinkled over with a big pinch of dried *herbes de provence*, and drank half a pint of milk in a single swig.

Dad I need you herlp

Ned was messaging again, asking for more money. Andrew tried to work up some urgency, but he kept staring into space, fixating on scenes that rose up at him from the night before.

Colleen standing on a table and singing an impassioned version of 'Like a Virgin' [or was it 'Don't You Want Me Baby?'? Possibly both].

Colleen fixing him with her fiery eyes and spitting venomous if familiar words at him: *It's all about you I gave you everything you're so weak I want to puke it's your fault we lost him.* Things like that.

Slow alcoholic kisses. Cries and arched backs, a tumble of hair. Gasps and whispers, the calling of names. Citrus scent and delirious body heat.

He loved her rage at these times, loved to take the full brunt of her, to live at the eye of her storm. Sex like fighting, then a sensuous, tender calm. And he was pretty sure that he in his turn had loved her in the old way, *with adoration, with fertile tears, with groans that thunder love, with sighs of fire.* It might have been nice if he could have remembered a bit more of it all, but still.

They had drunk. They had put music on, loud. Colleen had shouted at him. He had shouted back. He had called her a 'control fiend', an 'interfering bitch', a – of all things – 'menstrual tyrant'. [He was very disappointed with himself for the casual sexism of that one. Did one reveal one's true self in one's cups? Feelings that craved to be expressed, sure, but no doubt exaggerated, distorted, parodied even, under the influence. When you're angry, you reach for something to throw. But: a *menstrual* tyrant? I mean, *I'm a Guardian subscriber, for God's sake!*]

Looking into the bathroom mirror, he examined the gash on his forehead with a detached curiosity. He'd cracked his head on the hard glass corner of the nightstand. Hadn't even noticed at the time.

The inside-outsideness of our sex. You-in-me and me-in-you. They'd fucked like they were fighting, like in the good old days. Perfidious symmetry dared him to add that they had fought like they were fucking. But this, alas, was not the case. They may have fucked like they were fighting . . . but they had fought like they wanted to kill each other. Well, Colleen had. He mostly just tried to block and parry her attacks, in the interests of self-defence.

How wilt this fadge? The night just gone had left him bruised and exhilarated and hollow with self-loathing. He could taste and smell her still, even though his nostrils were now singed with the petrol tang of booze. But then the two smells, booze and Colleen, were not exactly incompatible.

No doubt it cut both ways. *You always taste of booze,* she had said to him once, about twenty-five years ago. *It's such a turn-on.*

He sat staring at the crossword, looking but seeing nothing, enjoying the winded silence, clinging to the ringing stillness.

B-R-I-D-A-L T-R-A-I-N

There was a pleasure here in this nothing, so long as he didn't move, so long as he didn't ever have to move again. When he moved his head, his whole brain jangled, so he wouldn't move his head, ever again. Now: if he could just still his anxious racing heart, subdue his raging thoughts, quench the burning nausea . . . A prayer to 'the Virgin for those who have nobody with', as the drunken Consul [his favourite literary booze-hound] pleads in *Under the Volcano*, and all might yet be forgiven him. He was on holiday, after all. Nothing was required of him. Colleen was out for the foreseeable. Ned, well, he lacked the energy or the will to respond to Ned right now. *Nothing will come of nothing*, he barded.

'Hello, hello! Does the master of the house have his trousers on? Hands off cocks, on with socks, as we used to say in the Navy. Ha ha!'

Oh, Jesus Christ. Not Wolf. Wolf was the last shitting thing.

III. HAIR OF THE DOG

While the cottage had been updated in a bland, contemporary style, the interior of the main Wolf house continued the traditional 'just-like-Grandma' theme established by the garden. It was a home that did not appear to have been updated in any way since it was first built a good 150 years ago.

The whole of the ground floor seemed to have retained its original tiling, a little cracked in paces, but wonderfully patterned and, uh, *characterful*. (If a little chilly in the winter, perhaps – despite the rugs everywhere.) There was a grandfather clock in the hall; there were displays of brass horse things and prints of the village from a hundred years ago and framed displays of old cigarette cards in the kitchen. (Colleen remembered these fondly; her own grandad used to collect them.) There were large ceramic and terracotta vases everywhere, most with arrangements of dried grasses in; some were as tall as a small child.

The house had big windows everywhere, but these were framed by heavy velvet curtains and further obscured by fussy lace screens. Jack's presence was everywhere, in the form of half-chewed bones, rope toys, and food and water bowls, not to mention the ever-present and unavoidable smell of dog, not exactly unpleasant but not exactly – on a morning like this morning – conducive to non-barfing either.

Wolf greeted his wife's guest warmly, clapping a harmless hand on her arm and steering her along a surprisingly long, tiled corridor to a set of steps at the back of the house. Along the way, Colleen passed open doors, through which she peered and became vaguely aware of a blur of polished knick-knacks, period tables, upholstered footrests. Another smell began to blend in with Jack's, which was probably furniture polish and/or Brasso. She sensed this was a house where a lot of shining of old tat took place.

The back room of the house where she ended up must have been the scullery that Andrew had described, the place where he had seen the Wolfs in full deviant flow. There was a big dresser, a couple of deep sinks, an incongruously modern double freezer – one of those with an ice cube dispenser in the door, Colleen noted with a small stab of envy – and a big oak table with benches. From this room, double doors opened out onto a slightly sunken patio area.

Looking around this scene of settled domestic harmony, Andrew's description of the Wolfs beating each other up seemed utterly impossible to believe. Had he been drinking that night? she wondered now. Did he make up the story to cover up his own drunkenness or something? She didn't think so, but then, she didn't see how it could be true either.

Outside, in the sunshine, Mrs Wolf – Hildy, or Hildi? – sat beckoning and smiling from her wheelchair at a wrought-iron garden table. A glass of something long and refreshing – lemonade? A spritzer? – sat at her elbow, along-side an elegant silver pot of coffee. As she got nearer, Colleen's heart leapt when she saw an ice bucket containing an unopened bottle of prosecco, with two flutey glasses on standby. It was a bit early, and she still felt very rough, but, well . . . hair of the dog and all that.

'Come here, my dear!' called Hildy, arms outstretched. 'Can you do the honours for me?' She gestured at the bubbly. Colleen leant across to give Hildy a peck on the cheek, as she was clearly expected to do, and started picking at the wire and foil seal. Her hands shook and she tutted to herself; though she could open a beer bottle with her teeth if she had to, this pressurised cork-popping business was always Andrew's department.

'Now then,' said Hildy – as they settled down at the table, and the opening exchange of pleasantries had been despatched with, and there had just been an agreeable pause in the conversation where each had sat back and looked out over the garden, taking in the pretty fluttery play of butter-flies on nasturtiums, and the darting of tits and warblers on the feeders, and there was a wonderful feeling when you just closed your eyes and you could feel the sun's rays actually warming your lids, not unpleasantly but more like a sort of blessing – 'Your Andrew.'

'Yes?' said Colleen.

'Does he have a big one?'

IV. A COUPLE TOO MANY

'That's a nasty scratch you've picked up there, old man,' said Wolf, with a chuckle that annoyed Andrew: there was too much enjoyment in it. Wolf had put down a packet of Lurpak on the table, and was now sitting down, swigging yet another cup of coffee. ['Lightly salted', the butter packet said, in what Andrew saw now was an early example of the dreaded artisanal brand voice that was now so trendy with soi-disant gourmet food brands and eateries. The insistence that everything had been produced with exquisite care, following time-honoured methods, using only the freshest ingredients, just like in the old country etc etc. 'Gently pan-fried by hand in the traditional manner'; well, sure, but how else are you going to cook a burger?]

Wolf perhaps thought Andrew was staring at the butter itself, rather than the packet's phraseology, for he added, 'I noticed you were short of butter, so I picked you up a pack.' [The butter, as far as Andrew recalled, was still in the bedroom, for reasons that remained blurry.]

'Oh,' he said. 'Thanks very much.' Andrew struggled to summon up some grateful feeling or other, but he was too busy just coping with feeling nothing. He was dimly aware of hoping that the subject of the big cut on his forehead had been and gone, gratefully superseded by the butter news. But he saw now that Wolf was staring at it anew with the intensity of a forensic investigator.

My own sweet crash scene, he thought.

'Now . . . how did you do that, I wonder?' said Wolf, whistling a mirthless little ditty through his teeth. It was a question aimed only at himself. Wolf was in high troubleshooting mode, with the same expression of gleeful clue-sniffing he wore when investigating Andrew's engine or the broadband issue. It was clear that Andrew was not invited to offer any input, only to provide an audience for Wolf's ponderings.

123

'Let me see . . . Perhaps you bumped it as you were opening the car boot. I've done that before, it swings out further than you realise and then . . . oof!!'

Andrew couldn't bring himself to move his head. 'Actually, I . . .' he began, but Wolf cut him off.

'Or perhaps you were groping around in the cupboard under the stairs, looking for something, maybe the recycling bin so you could stash some of those empties. Yes! That's it! You forget to switch the light on – it's outside on the wall, remember – but you carry on in the dark, until you catch your head on the sloping bit of the ceiling . . .'

Andrew failed to move his head again. It seemed they were playing some sort of game. He didn't even bother trying to reply this time.

'Ouch!' Wolf giggled, even more pleased with himself. 'Or wait! . . . Maybe you'd had a couple too many, and you were a little unsteady on your feet. You went to get some bottles from the garden but you tripped on the step coming out of the back door, and you fell into the rockery!'

'Uh.' [Although: What were he and Colleen if not *a couple too many?*]

'Oh, come on!' said Wolf encouragingly. 'We've all done it. We've all been young once. Not that you are, any more, not exactly.'

This was true. Andrew didn't move his head again.

'Or maybe . . .' said Wolf relentlessly. 'Aha! Ach, so! Maybe there was pleasure before the pain.'

Andrew looked up at him, startled.

'Yes! Ja! So maybe . . . you banged your head in the throes of erotic abandon.'

Andrew stared at him wildly.

'In which case,' Wolf sailed on regardless, 'I'm sure it was worth it. Now sire, get your boots on – we're off to Tony's.'

They drove in silence. Andrew toyed with a few words and phrases in his mind, but the idea of making them flesh and setting them to live in the tortuous interjective space between himself and Wolf seemed hopelessly far-fetched. What, really, did he want to say anyway? And why did he have to tax himself with such complexities, at a time when talk of any kind was so difficult?

It was odd, of course it was, that Wolf had guessed that his minor head injury was sex-related. But odder still, perhaps, was the fact that, to the best of his memory, all of the other scenarios that Wolf had outlined with such enjoyment had also happened to him last night.

Wolf was spying on him. This was bad.

But now Andrew would be expected – even by himself – to do something about it. This was worse.

V. THE CONSEQUENCES OF THINGS

He was so funny he took her breath away.

That was how Colleen always remembered Andrew, back in the old days. Back when they were 'courting' (as Hildy kept calling it).

She met Andrew in a pub. She was actually out with Gerry that night, and the three of them ended up part of a small group that had formed around a quiz machine. Andrew, of course, knew all the answers. She was still trying to make her drama career work at the time. Gerry had found her a part in an earnest new play about the Chartists. It was '*off*-off West End', as they liked to call it. There was no money in it, but she was in the theatre and loving it all.

Andrew always said afterwards that he just *knew* the moment he saw her. It took her about twenty-four hours longer. He joined their group, and they went on to another pub. Gerry got distracted by someone he bumped into that he knew from somewhere else – that always happened with

Gerry – so she was left on her own with this quietly spoken, nerdish figure with the surprising sense of humour.

Andrew had been so funny that night. He did crap impressions, told confessional stories with himself as the butt of the joke. They walked along lamplit streets, staggering with laughter, making instant memories. They met again at a party, the next weekend, which was where it had all really begun.

'Ooh!' put in Hildy, topping up Colleen's bubbly. 'So he laughed you into bed, did he?'

'Pretty much,' Colleen had to agree.

The first time had been awful of course, she recalled, careful not to mention this bit to Hildy. But there was something so playful and endearing about him that she had consented to see him again. And then, suddenly, they became, sort of, *addicted* to each other.

Andrew would turn up at her flat in the middle of the night. She'd let him in, and they'd do it right there on the stairs. They did it at other people's house parties, on trains, at the back of a National Express coach once, which took some doing. (They even managed it at her parents' house a couple of times, which – given her mum's extreme traditional views about sex outside of marriage – was without doubt their most daring erotic feat of all.)

They were always sneaking off to have sex, she recalled, always trying stuff out. Soon after they met, Andrew had to return to Luxembourg, where he was completing a technical translation course. She turned up at his place one night out of the blue. He did the same to her a few times – in London, at the Edinburgh Festival. It got to the point where if one of them had to go off somewhere, they'd actually be surprised and a little disappointed if the other didn't show up unannounced for some clandestine and inventive intercourse.

Oh Lord. What was that all about? It's only sex, for God's sake.

There was something compulsive about it all. They needed to keep drinking in the other, and each stunt had to outdo the previous one. They kept bits of each other, they made a fetish of each other's bodies. She had a lock of his hair, she slept in an old T-shirt of his that she never washed; he had pics and things of hers. Thank God there were no camera phones about when they were courting, Colleen thought suddenly. God knows what sort of stuff they would have sent each other. At one point there had been outfits and props, she vaguely recalled. But they'd only been playing, really. Other people's sex lives are probably as boring from the outside as other people's dreams. Or other people's holiday pics. But at the time, my God.

The sad part, of course, was that there was no way this sort of intensity could endure. The only way was down. Life got in the way, it wasn't always possible to get away, or maybe the allure of secret rendezvous was gradually offset by the expense and the inconvenience. And in any case, before they had time to be disappointed about the cooling of their passion, they were living together and she was pregnant with the twins.

And by then, there was so much else to deal with, so much else to be disappointed by.

When she first met Andrew she was living the dream. She'd put a play on, she was getting acting parts, she was going for auditions. She was writing and directing and going into schools and running Shakespeare workshops. She was making no money, of course, but she had so much energy and passion and had set so many irons in the fire . . . Surely one of these had to lead to something eventually?

Andrew was with her every step of the way, to start with. He came along to the shows. He helped out painting scenery and scouring second-hand shops for props. He was a tireless

127

rehearser of lines, a creative sounding board – even, on occasion, a one-man standing ovation.

He loved her passion. He read her poetry in the bath. He grew flowers for her in their little garden. He liked to turn up at the theatre with his home-made 'rehearsal survival kit' – typically Polos, Hula Hoops, a pre-mixed G&T and a *Guardian* crossword.

But then: the sell-out. A couple of Colleen's drama school friends had got involved with a training company that ran courses for marketers and businesspeople in things like time management and assertiveness at work and presentation skills. They told Colleen she'd be ideal for it, they were always looking for new trainers.

Colleen went along to an interview, and before she knew it she was co-facilitating a session on Building Your Confidence in Groups. She was a natural: she knew it, and they knew it. They offered her a job the next day. But when the frisson of surprise and self-congratulation subsided, she began to have doubts.

It would only be for a few months, she told herself. It was good money – especially for an impoverished actor – and she could use it to help support her drama projects. She'd carry on as much of the theatre stuff as she could, until she'd saved up a bit. That was how she saw it, and how Andrew encouraged her to see it. He was starting to make some decent money from his translating work, and he'd subbed them both pretty much, up till then. So perhaps she felt a certain pressure to pay her way? (Ironically it seemed to be more and more the other way round these days, she wasn't sure why.)

So: it would only be for a little while. Except that before she knew it, Colleen was taken on as a permanent member of staff. Suddenly she was a knackered stay-at-home mum of two terrifyingly helpless twin babies, drunk with tiredness and covered in sick. (Andrew had done his bit, of course, except when he hadn't.) And then, when she looked up, it was three and a half years later, and she was back at the company earning easy money again, and the idea of returning to the theatre now looked like someone else's fast-receding pipe dream, haltingly glimpsed in a misted-up rear-view mirror.

It was hard not to blame him. Andrew was supposed to know her better than she knew herself. He was supposed to keep her focused on the things she really cared about, even – especially – when she threatened to sabotage her own dreams. But when she'd come to that fork in the road, he'd let her take the easy route, the one that led to comfort and security and cash ISAs and self-loathing and no way back.

Privately, she called it The Great Betrayal. It wasn't his only one, and it wasn't even the worst, but it had the terrible distinction of being the first.

The bubbly was slipping down a treat, and as the afternoon slipped away with it Colleen found it hard to tell the difference between the bits she was recalling to herself and the bits she was saying out loud. Her natural urge to be discreet about her marital sex life was coming under fierce and relentless pressure from Hildy, who knew no subtlety or tact whatsoever and just kept badgering you for intimate details, and of course you were too hungover and tipsy to resist for long and so in the end you just told her whatever she wanted and God knows what else besides.

'I wouldn't say it was especially long,' she heard herself saying, in response to a question she had been too surprised to answer before. 'But it does have the advantage of a certain *girth*.'

The use of the word 'girth' in this context was so amusing to Hildy that Colleen thought her companion was about to have an aneurysm. But it was fun to laugh and be naughty, and not think for a while about the consequences of things. And so together they giggled their way through the afternoon. It was easier that way.

VI. NOW AND NEVER

Tony proved to be a corpulent old rocker with a gnarled shaven head, a Lemmy-style handlebar moustache and two blunt fistfuls of sovereign rings. He wore a cut-off denim jacket over an old black T-shirt that bore the tour dates of some band with an umlaut over an impossible vowel. [Always a bad sign, mused Andrew.] His stubby legs, meanwhile, were squeezed into a pair of eye-wateringly tight leather trousers. What looked like a large silver cast of a shark's tooth hung on a leather strap around his neck, and a big thick pirate's earring swung proudly from each lobe. The whole effect, Andrew decided, was almost, but not quite, camp.

Wolf and Tony shook hands with great solemnity, as if they were the sort of men – or so it seemed to Andrew – who went about their business like ordinary people by day, but belonged by night to a secret fraternity that went out killing certain segments of the population for compelling ideological reasons that were darkly connected to alt.right conspiracy theories, then burying them in unmarked graves in the woods. [*Paranoid: moi?*] The pair disappeared into Tony's office, a rickety shed that sat at the back of his yard, overseeing the cars and pickups – and even a tractor – in their various states of disrepair.

Behind this shed-office, Andrew noticed a breeze-block lock-up with a car jacked up high on a, well, on a jack thing, beneath which a younger man, stripped to the waist, was attending greasily to the underside. Andrew took this lad for Tony's son, doubtless a recent initiate into the murderous confraternity, entrance to which he must have secured, to his father's great pride, by passing a rite involving the intra-venous ingestion of crystal meth and the sacrificial stabbing of a vagrant.

They drove back to the cottage in silence, with Wolf and Tony in the front, and Andrew sitting in the back like the family dog. Tony sprawled in the front passenger seat with obscene self-confidence, the force of his relentless personal-ity encroaching on Andrew's timid airspace as he leaned back in his seat and Andrew felt the pressure on his legs with every shift of self-satisfied bodyweight. Every so often Wolf would point to a house on the route, and Tony would snicker. These homes doubtless contained the families of targets for their death-metal, alt.right, Satan cult, though whether past or future victims it was hard to discern.

Andrew knew there was something he should be thinking hard about, but the intrusion of Tony into the scene drowned out all other possible thinking. After an initial nod so undemonstrative as to seem positively hostile, Tony had since said nothing to Andrew, barely acknowledged his pres-ence. In a way this suited Andrew in his current state even if it was at the same time a bit odd, especially given that it was Andrew's car that Tony was supposed to be mending, and Andrew who would presumably be paying him. [Unless of course Wolf had told him otherwise; really, he was utterly in their hands.]

When they got back to Wolf's, Andrew went inside the cottage to make them all a hot drink. There was still no sign of Colleen, he noted with a pang. Tony and Wolf, meanwhile, immediately pulled up the bonnet and set to poking and pointing at the engine. Andrew wasn't sure how long this went on for – he was detained by a period of inert stupor at one point, and then called away by the urgent need for a massive dump, during which he ran through his mnemonics for German prepositions and the cases that govern

131

them – but certainly he had to re-boil the kettle a couple of times. By the time he emerged with the mugs on a tray – an attractive circular wooden one, with a picture of a woman kissing a man, only when you look closer you can see she is carrying a book under her arm called *Easy ways to Murder your Husband*, while he has a dagger behind his back, and is grinning for the camera with an evil glint in his eye – Tony was driving off again. At the sight of Andrew, he wound down his window.

'Sorry!' said Andrew. 'I've got your drink here.'

'Not a worry,' said Tony, with the grave air of a man who has in his time sacrificed many mugs of tea.

'Is everything . . . ? Er, about . . . the car?'

'It's the upper transponder,' said Wolf from behind him, with a sad shake of his head.

'Off for the part now,' said Tony.

And with that his tyres skidded deftly on the gravel and he was back out on the road before Andrew could ask, 'Is that serious?' or 'How much might that be?' or 'How long will that take?' or even 'What is an upper transponder – and is this a worse scenario than one involving the lower transponder?'

Wolf stood with a proprietorial hand on the Astra's bonnet, savouring his coffee and patting Jack's head.

'He's a good old boy, that Tony,' he said at last.

'Thanks for putting us in touch with him,' said Andrew helplessly. In the depths of the Wolf house, he could hear Colleen and Mrs Wolf beginning their goodbyes. There seemed to be a surprising amount of shrieking and squawking involved.

He had to say something to Wolf. And this was the moment, wasn't it? On he pondered with painful prevarication, more Hamlet than Hamlet. Yet again he wondered: why did *now* and *never* have to be such aggressively binary options?

VII. AN ENTIRELY VOLUNTARY ARRANGEMENT

After they'd had the twins, Colleen was now prompted by Hildy to recall, Andrew was going to do the Daddy Daycare thing. Once the children were in pre-school, he would scale back on his work, so she could get back to hers. The training company was happy for her to work whatever hours suited her and to pay her well, but in a way this didn't help: it gave Andrew an excuse to just go along with the status quo, a situation in which she still did the bulk of the childcare and he ran away from any change or extra work that would threaten his own precious routines.

He took to going out to work in the office of an agency that gave him regular work. This was an entirely voluntary arrangement, but suddenly Andrew – the man who had insisted he could never work in an office again, the man who said he couldn't wait to become a proper stay-at-home dad while his wife strutted her stuff upon the stage – was in there all the time. He was subtle about it, but underneath the stealth there was extraordinary stubbornness too.

He would shuffle off to 'his office', claiming he had to show his face for an important client meeting, and end up staying out till after the pick-up time for the kids, after their food time and . . . 'Oh God, sorry love, I got pulled into another thing. There's a new project that's kicking off, could be really big, and they want a transcreator in at the start of it' – and of course, by the time he got home, there was just time for him to pop up and kiss the dear sweet heads of his little twins.

Sometimes, if they were really lucky (and if they were still awake) Daddy might even deign to read them a story. So Colleen sat and seethed downstairs, nursing a large spritzer, while Andrew performed *We're Going on a Bear Hunt* or *Duck in a Truck* with dazzling verve and multiple voices and . . . *Daddy you're so funny! Can you take us in to pre-school tomorrow?*

Good old funny old Daddy. Then she would have to come up and explain that it was time to turn the lights off or they wouldn't cope tomorrow, and fun-times Dad would nod sadly and they would all regretfully yield once more to the dull-but-sensible naggings of boring old killjoy Mummy, and then Mum and Dad would pad downstairs for a glass of wine, and Andrew would be sniffing about the kitchen and asking what's for dinner and saying, *Wow, what a day I had,* and looking at her flushed from the success of his latest performance with the kids with a face that seemed to say, *I'm sorry, love; I guess I just can't help being the hilarious, effortlessly charismatic one,* and she would look at him as if to say, *Guess what? I'd be a lot more fun if I wasn't left with sole responsibility for them every single day,* and *I guess you just can't help being a self-centred shit.*

Slowly and stubbornly, over that period of time that parents of young children experience as simultaneously glacial, blurry, stolen and agonisingly stressful, Andrew quietly dug himself in, entrenching his own position as the one who had options and autonomy and time for himself, and in the process quietly treading all over her dreams.

But that was just it, of course. That, perhaps, was what she held against him most of all.

Andrew had never really had a dream.

VIII. HOT LAWYER LETTING HAIR DOWN

'Wolf!' Andrew called after the retreating figure. Colleen and Hildy had still not emerged. The pair seemed to be caught in an ecstasy of leave-taking. The moment was still here to be seized, dammit.

'Yes, old boy?' Wolf turned, with almost implausible responsiveness, as if he had been waiting for Andrew to call him back.

'How did you know all that stuff about me banging my head and that?'

'Oh, did I hit the target? I'm getting good at that game.'

'It was more than a guess though, wasn't it?'

'*Hot lawyer letting hair down,*' said Wolf.

'You what?'

'*Tattoo on inner thigh.*'

'I . . .'

'*Evil stepmother goddess bitch + leather.*'

'You . . .'

'Sorry. *+ hot.*'

'Wolf.'

'*Wet play. Women kissing.*'

Andrew walked away. He walked away because Wolf wouldn't stop.

He walked away because Colleen would be out soon, and he thought Wolf might stop if he wasn't there to hear him.

He walked away because if Wolf wouldn't stop, then at least he wouldn't have to listen to him.

He walked away because if he wouldn't stop, then at least Andrew wouldn't have to watch Colleen hearing him.

He walked away because the Google search phrases that Wolf was spouting were all ones that he already knew only too well.

IX. THE WOK OF MORAL SUPERIORITY

Colleen returned to the cottage carrying the spare bottle of bubbles that Hildy had insisted she take with her.

'Share some with hubby,' she cooed. 'Go back to bed, the pair of you. Brighten up the rest of the day!'

Had she over-shared with Hildy? she wondered now with a stab of remorse. Almost certainly. But the bubbles had been going down a treat, Hildy was relentless, and she had lost track of what she was saying, and she knew there were indiscretions she would regret later. But she was pleasantly afloat, drifting clear of sobriety for another day, and it was hard to regard anything with much seriousness just now.

Back in the cottage, Andrew was busy making a stir-fry for dinner. Andrew's cooking was always nakedly connected to his state of mind. If he was trying to say sorry or repair a row, he'd be knocking up kedgeree or shepherd's (NEVER cottage!) pie, since these were among his wife's official favourites. If he thought there was a chance of romance, he'd be frying fancy steaks or faffing around with something French, like coq au vin. If he was trying to knock the booze on the head for a few days, feeling guilty about recent excesses and trying to get him (and her) back on the road to clean living, he would inevitably reach – as he was doing now – for his stir-fry option.

Stir-fry was low in fat and easy to prepare, she knew he thought. He found virtue in the chopping of vegetables, the minimal cooking time, the simplicity and earnestness of the ingredients. It was also as boring as anything to eat, she thought, suddenly an expert at twisting the wire off the bottle top, unwrapping the foil and removing the cork without wasting a drop. But at least she knew where his head was at.

Was there another bottle of Abs left in the cupboard in the utility room? She would need to check later. Also, she felt a sudden need to check outside the back door for her little stray. Perhaps not a kitten after all, but an accidental miniature. A free spirit of the woods who lived off his charm, she fancied.

'Fancy a drop?'

Andrew looked across at her with a disdain that he made a poor show of concealing. She had a flash memory of slapping him across the face last night, and a sudden urge to do it again. Look at him with his wok of moral superiority, sneering down at her from his soy-sauce high ground! *He* could talk. He'd been worse than her last night. Necking it down like there was no tomorrow. Staggering about the place like a drunken buffoon. Badgering her for sex.

She shouldn't have slept with him. It would only give him ideas. She'd been seized by the moment. They were well-practised in the sex, and if you weren't careful it was easy to let the old habits kick in. But it never fixed anything. Men always thought it did, but it didn't. Just the opposite, in fact.

'I thought today we might have an evening off the sauce,' said Andrew pointedly. 'But I see you're already under way.'

'We've been doing that all week, thanks to that bloody email from the Pauls,' she said. 'And where did it get us?'

Andrew put the plates down on the table. He positioned the paper between them, open at the cryptic crossword – another of his standard couple-therapy gestures.

They ate for a while in silence. Colleen stared moodily at the clues.

'You bastard!' she said at last. 'You filled in 17 across!'

Andrew looked at the puzzle. 'B-R-I-D-A-L T-R-A-I-N,' he read.

'I was about to work that out!' It was a lie, of course, they both knew it. But it was nice to have something concrete to blame him for.

Andrew looked at her and at the paper again. He looked puzzled.

'I never wrote that in,' he said quietly.

'Of course you did!' she said. Jesus, she was feeling light-headed already. Maybe a bath in a minute?

'No,' he said with a quiet firmness that she knew was truthful. 'I didn't.'

'Oh, don't be ridiculous,' she said anyway. 'If *you* didn't fill it in . . . and *I* didn't . . .'

Outside they heard a dog barking, accompanied by some relentlessly cheerful whistling.

Andrew said, 'I'll give you one guess.' As their eyes met, she wondered if he too felt for a moment like they were in an episode of *Scooby-Doo*.

'By the way, did I tell you about the grave in the woods? And is there any more of this?' said Andrew, draining the last of the prosecco into a pint glass.

THURSDAY

don't know where to start. it all went so wrong
always thought it would turn around on its own
all so fucked
don't blame yourselves, you each have your way
if only you knew – the fight it takes to finish one day
wishing there won't be another
dreams of a different tomorrow
dreams of home

I. MY WEAKNESS IS MY STRENGTH

After breakfast, Colleen holed up in the bathroom again, more scent and bubbles no doubt, while Andrew wondered whether he should wander outside and give Wolf a piece of his mind. At last. Once and for all. *Now.*

Wolf had been spying on them, there was no other word for it. He'd obviously got hold of Andrew's phone at some point, because he seemed to know his recent search history and somehow knew about him messaging Ned. He'd been in the cottage when they were out, nosing in cupboards and noting missing ingredients and filling in people's crossword clues [an oddly intimate violation of their *privacy*]. [And wasn't it interesting to note, incidentally, that British people pronounced it less and less often /ˈprɪvəsi/ but increasingly preferred /ˈpraɪvəsi/ which pronunciation, originally American he fancied, has the effect of highlighting the sound of 'I', the first-person pronoun and obvious injured party.]

Wolf was obviously snooping round the house at all hours, looking in windows and eavesdropping on conversations, because he had the low-down on pretty much everything they'd been up to, everything that had gone on between them. [If Andrew was honest with himself, and to complete the charge sheet, he was also a tiny bit peeved that Wolf had feigned incomprehension when he'd tried out his German on him. *Das ist ausgezeichnet, nicht wahr?* he'd exclaimed in reaction to a positive bulletin about progress on the car-fixing front. But Wolf had ignored him completely, perhaps inflicting thereby the teensiest wound to Andrew's *amour-propre* while no doubt affording the older man some small degree of *Schadenfreude.*]

Anyhow, someone with any courage or backbone would surely have confronted Wolf by now, wouldn't they? Colleen's perpetual charge of cowardice rang loud in his head. But what was he going to do – physically threaten an old man? Andrew had never physically threatened anyone in his life; it seemed wrong now to begin with a late septuagenarian. [He himself was an early quinquagenarian, of course, which also seemed quite late to be starting with the threatening.] Also, confronting Wolf would incur the risk of certain people finding out about other stuff i.e. Ned [a late vicenarian, fyi]. Could he take that risk? Don't even ask.

Andrew sifted the evidence. He stood in the back garden, sipping a coffee and waiting for someone to tell him what to do, for something to react to.

As I am man, my state is desperate for my master's love . . .

As I am woman, now alas the day!

What thriftless sighs shall Olivia breathe . . .

Involving Colleen was a high-risk option in any case. Yes, she would no doubt be shocked and appalled by the snooping. Yes, he could get her on side against Wolf, up to a point. True too, the search phrases were embarrassing. But if Wolf had been able to access those – and so much for the so-called 'private browsing mode' on his devices, by the way! – there were, he knew, other search terms that he'd be even less comfortable to see aired. 'Signs you're bi' was an obvious one. 'Concealing payments from a joint account' would be another.

The very worst thing, of course, was that Wolf knew about his contact with Ned. His ongoing payments to Ned were a secondary secret, one that Colleen would probably guess for herself were she to be apprised of the devastating primary deception – the fact of Andrew still being in communication with their son. A fact that was in direct contravention of the strictest rule between them. Funnily enough, he felt there was a different tone to some of Ned's most recent messages, something about dreaming of home and wondering where it all went wrong, and he yearned to share this with Colleen. But then, as she would no doubt remind him, their hopes had been crushed so many times before.

They had appeased Ned's addiction time and again, after all, made excuses for him, blamed themselves, extended to him so many *one more chances* and stays of execution, paid for expensive rehab courses and therapists and alternative treatment centres. They locked him in his room, took away his phone, staged interventions, but still they always ended up issuing apologies and making reparations on his behalf to all the people whose promises he broke, whose money he stole, whose children he led astray.

All the people they knew about anyway. Just like when he was a child, Ned went on leaving a trail of chaos in his wake. And just like when he was a child, they followed behind, cursing and sighing and playing the part of long-suffering passive-aggressive parents to the hilt as they cleared up the mess.

Only the stakes got much higher, and the mess much messier.

Colleen, who spoke to experts and read every book and went completely teetotal during this period, argued that cutting Ned off completely was his only chance of breaking free of smack or crystal or spice or whatever he was now into. So long as he had his mum and dad as a safety net, however unwilling or punitive they tried to be about it, Ned would never hit rock bottom, she argued. And so long as Ned never hit rock bottom, he would never confront his addiction. The danger, of course, was that he might die before – or as – he hit rock bottom, but desperate times called for desperate measures.

Colleen was probably right. There was a sort of controlled fury about the way she followed through on the plan. She told Andrew that if he couldn't get behind her on this, then she couldn't see a way forward for them to stay together. She made him give up the booze too. They made a solemn vow – a vow as solemn as their marriage vow, as she put it – to stick to the cut-off, whatever Ned did or said to get them to take pity on him, whatever ruses he pulled to get them to lower their defences once more – compassion being, Colleen reminded him forcefully, just another word for enablement in this toxic context.

'You've got to be extra vigilant,' she told him. 'You're the one who's more likely to crack, so he'll work on you first.'

Andrew protested; Andrew equivocated; Andrew conceded. Andrew played his part. He made the pledge, changed the locks, packed Ned's stuff. Colleen drove her only son to a sort of halfway hostel place where he could get some help if he chose. He wouldn't, of course; they both knew he wouldn't.

Andrew offered to do that final drive, but Colleen said she couldn't trust him to see it through. He'd probably end up giving Ned the car or making some dodgy agreement to keep on subbing him under the radar. [How well she knew him.] But the look she gave him as she took the key from its hook and led Ned out to the car was a look he would have paid good money never to have been on the end of.

It wasn't long after Ned left [for good?] that Colleen began drinking again. In the evenings she'd take to opening up a bottle as soon as she got in, and then she'd just carry on the rest of the night. She never drank on a school night, mind, she was very strict about that. But then she managed to condense her working week so she had fewer and fewer school nights. Colleen told Andrew it was to free up more time to work on the book – a book she'd never even started, as far as he knew – but the new arrangement basically increased the number of nights she could booze with impunity every week.

And of course, he'd just gone along with that too. It was just another way his weakness had led him to appease her. She drank, so he drank, to keep her company. To keep an eye on her really, just to stay with her. He could stop tomorrow, if it was just down to him. Yet here he was, terrified of his wife finding out about him enabling his addict son – while his addict wife effectively carried on insisting that he enable *her.*

Come on. Are you a man or a mouse? Quelle honte.

He couldn't even just get in the car and drive away from it all, not when the car wouldn't start. They were prisoners of Ned's addiction, prisoners of Wolf's surveillance, prisoners of his passivity and lack of practical nous. He used to confess to Colleen, a long time ago, his fears of not being brave or bold enough to be a man, of not knowing how he'd react if he were put to the test. But she soothed him and reassured him. *Your 'weakness' is your strength,* she told him. She meant he had other qualities that more than compensated – his humour, his empathy, his sensitivity – and that there was a bravery in his honesty. And anyway, she was lioness enough for the both of them, wasn't she? For a wife to say, *Why can't you be more of a man?* was as outdated as a husband saying, *It's about time you acted like a wife!* In later years, however, this very nuanced and heartfelt position of Colleen's had modulated into something less subtle, something that might be succinctly summarised as: *Why do you have to be such a bloody pussy?*

And of course, pussy that he was, he tended to agree with her.

My weakness is my strength.

Unfortunately, my weakness is also my weakness.

II. THE HUMAN EQUIVALENT OF A SWISS ARMY KNIFE

When Colleen stirred from her post-bath nap, she could tell by a certain quality in the light peeping round the edges of her curtained window that it was still depressingly early outside. Well, and inside. The digital figures on her alarm beeped a banal 10:23. In her mind's eye, she saw the rest of this, what – Thursday? Friday? Wednesday? – stretched out before her in a long conveyor belt of dead hours.

She felt jet-lagged, as if she had gone to sleep in one time zone and woken in another. The whole week was a bit like this. First off, they'd been trying so hard and not drinking and sitting on beaches, and now they were not trying so hard and not sitting on beaches, and having the odd drink, and of course everything was much more relaxed, albeit still rather boring.

She sensed that Andrew was not in the house. He was up and about somewhere, perhaps trying to see about the car yet again, or else pacing the meadow to get his steps in.

Jack barked happily outside. Say what you like about Hildy and Wolf, it was touching how they looked out for each other, out here in the middle of nowhere. There was a sort of *chivalry* about Wolf's devotion to his wife. Something you didn't really see any more. Hildy was outspoken and bossy, of course, and a bit of a lush. Also a sex maniac. The lines of her character had probably become more exaggerated now that she was stuck in a chair, but Wolf worked hard to let her carry on being her loud effusive self nonetheless.

Why was Hildy in a chair anyway? Colleen had a feeling that Hildy had indirectly explained what had happened at some point during their boozy tea, but she hadn't really taken it in. Did that grave in the woods have anything to do with it? Did they lose a baby? Colleen never mentioned it, and of course it would be beyond rude to ask again now. Maybe Andrew could subtly get the story out of Wolf?

Andrew was building up some serious moral outrage about the idea of Wolf sneaking around the house and snooping on them, but Colleen couldn't really see what the fuss was about. Here he was, stuck out in the woods with his incapacitated wife, nothing else to do but walk his dog and tend the little one's grave. Keeping a benevolent eye on his guests was probably about as much fun or interest as he had to look forward to. And really. It was only a crossword clue.

OK, it was a slightly mad and controlling sort of benevolent eye that Wolf kept on his guests, but still. There was a sort of practical, hands-on, old-school kindness to him too that was really very touching. Wolf got up and out and did stuff; he went out of his way to help. He wasn't passive, not like *some people*. In fact, it was as if he *needed* you to need him. OK, so maybe he had listened in on the odd conversation at the kitchen door, but if so he had only used that info to perform little favours for them – bringing in some butter they didn't need, two kinds of tea, the loan of an umbrella.

And then look at all the time and effort he was putting in to trying to get their car fixed. Admittedly it still wasn't fixed, judging from the strangulated ignition noises she could hear outside, but still.

Shall I have a drink? Maybe not.

He needs us to need him, she thought. I wonder where that comes from? Perhaps because of her work, Colleen liked to guess at the backstories of the people she came across. (Andrew liked to say that she was 'a sucker for the biological fallacy' or something – the idea that people can be explained by their pasts. Well, it sounded like a perfectly reasonable idea to her.) She imagined Wolf fleeing Germany as a young child in the aftermath of the Second World War, with the aid of a kindly English uncle perhaps. Parents lost in the bombings, a gaping absence in a row of terraced houses like a missing tooth, one small suitcase containing all he had, a card address label on a string, a little boy lost in cap and shorts. Trying so hard to fit in. A terrible immigrant childhood, constantly bullied by the other lads because of an accent which he just can't quite shake off.

Maybe later. Maybe not.

Or wait. Does he perhaps refuse to lose his accent, because it's all he has left of his past, a last link to his parents?

Maybe now.

Eventually, he learns that people won't be so cruel to you if you can be of service to them. And so he builds a personality that is the human equivalent of a Swiss Army knife. Wolf becomes the sort of man who can plaster a wall for you, fix your car (!), sort out your computer. You only have to mention you're going to Morocco on holiday, and he'll be round with a printout of the best things to see and do, a list of all the jabs you need, and the current temperature on the ground. He probably does a mean spaghetti bolognaise too.

'Say what you like about Wolf,' the lads at grammar school and later at work would say, 'But he's a useful bloke to know. *The fucking Nazi.*' They would have had it both ways, no doubt. But Wolf persisted. He had to; he was a survivor. This man who just by existing rubbed Germany in the face of every Brit he came across, who was a living reminder of the most hated thing in post-war British life, learned to make himself indispensable. If he could do something for you, it would be that bit harder to hate him. Poor love. What a life he must have led.

And then, she thought, a man like that, driven to make people like him . . . if you didn't offer something he could do for you, he would probably have to start proactively *looking for ways he could help*. The world was full of people who hadn't forgiven him yet. To appease them, he would offer a useful service or three. And if none was forthcoming, he might listen in or snoop around a little bit, until he found a way in which he could be of service.

Perhaps he even *exaggerated* the odd problem or two so he could be the one to help out? Was the car really so crocked that it needed all week to fix, for example – or was Wolf deliberately delaying things, just gearing up to demonstrate how indispensable he was? There was a glint of mischief in his eye, she often thought. It was what made his compulsive helpfulness so endearing, rather than needy and embarrassing.

Was there still some Chablis in the fridge?

Then Hildy. Had she been in a chair when she and Wolf first met? Definitely she had problems already, Colleen surmised, some sort of ongoing condition, probably something that was only going to get worse. That, of course, would have scared most men off. But in Wolf – wired as he was with an obsessive need to be of use – she had found the perfect match. Someone that needed him all the time. And so he became her sort of marital carer.

Of course, this would also explain the weird sex stuff. Hildy may have been ill, but she had clearly not lost her sexual appetite. (It seemed they'd had a child together, lost it very early on. Perhaps they lost it as a result of her illness?) If anything, Hildy's appetites seemed to intensify and get weirder, as Colleen had read somewhere could happen with certain psychological disorders. It was hard to know exactly how incapacitated she was, and where or why – both she and Wolf were very vague about this, and it wasn't exactly something you could press them about. But if Hildy now wasn't able (or willing?) to do some of the usual sexual stuff, she clearly got her rocks off by knocking Wolf about a bit – something he was probably programmed to enjoy, if Colleen's analysis of him was correct; it was just another way to serve. Plus of course, as Colleen knew only too well, she liked to ply passers-by with booze till they spilled the secrets of their own sex lives.

Well, why not? It was all harmless, really, wasn't it? A way for damaged people to make the best of things.

And then, a vile thought: perhaps Wolf had done something bad to put Hildy in the chair, so that she would be obliged to rely on him for the rest of her life? And what about the grave? Did the dog maul their baby on Wolf's watch? Is that why she punishes him still? (Her little stray must live in constant fear of Jack.)

OK, stop all this. But it was hard not to speculate on these dark things. It was these woods, and the unseasonal sultry weather, and Wolf's weirdness. Not to mention all the true-crime books. It got you wondering.

III. SHIBBOLETH

Andrew saw Wolf heading out with Jack for a walk in the quicksand woods. On an impulse, he slipped on his shoes and ran across the road to catch up with him.

This time, he would really have it out with Wolf. He'd give him bloody what-for. Wolf was going to sodding well *get it.*

'Ach, hello! So it is the master of the house! How are you, sir?'

Jack was barking excitedly to see Andrew, jumping up and running round and round him in tight delighted circles. Wolf, who had been striding hard, was panting a little from his exertions. Once again, Andrew had the sense of tremendous wiry energy from a man who must be – what – in his late seventies or early eighties at least? An old man to be hitting.

Andrew looked at Wolf expectantly, as if he expected Wolf to simply admit his misdemeanours, apologise for his wrongdoings, beg for forgiveness, vow to sin no more. But Wolf just looked back at him with his usual blithely comical sphinx face.

This was the trouble with wrongdoers and evil people in general. They never seemed to see what they had done as in any sense *wrong.* You could wait for ever for an admission of guilt from a guilty person. Did evil people even see themselves as evil? Do criminals ever self-identify as *criminals,* i.e. as people who have made a career out of breaking society's agreed rules of conduct? Or if they did refer to themselves as 'criminals', did they reframe the word to mean something more positive, even aspirational? Villain. Grifter. Chancer. *Outlaw.*

What a hopelessly middle-class train of thought. While he was running through the motions of this bollocks, another man [an actual man] would be chasing the offender down the street, or reaching for his air pistol.

'So you've been looking at my phone.' There was a tremor in his voice that he despised. But the words were out at least, and they were gratifyingly to the point.

Wolf did not appear remotely perturbed. 'Oh, you know. You leave things lying around . . . careless talk costs wives and all that.'

'Wives?' Andrew's heart leapt, and not pleasantly. Wolf seemed to have a heat-seeking missile for Andrew's every painful embarrassment or confusion. How did he do that?

'Your Colleen,' he was saying now. 'A fine woman.'

'What's she got to do with any of this?'

'Does she know about Ned?'

'Of course she does. She's his mum.'

'Ah,' said Wolf. 'But does she know you're still in touch with him?'

'—'

'Does she know you score for him sometimes? That you sit up chatting to him every night and sending him money?'

'—'

'Does she know he's been inside?'

'—'

Now Wolf put his face closer to Andrew's. *'Does she know about the foot?'*

Andrew stopped dead.

Wolf grinned. 'And do you know that she will find out about all these things unless you find a way to include the word "shibboleth" in conversation tomorrow?'

The foot. Andrew took a step back involuntarily. He felt winded, as if someone had just punched him very, very hard in the stomach when he was least expecting it. [Which, incidentally, was how Houdini died, wasn't it?] The air around him stung, his ears were ringing, the trees were not real. *Oh, Jesus God, the foot.*

Wolf was striding ahead now, a raised stick in one hand. Jack looked up at his owner with a happily expectant expression. Andrew found himself stumbling blindly after him.

'You're a lunatic! You're a fucking troll! A mentalist! What you're doing is completely illegal! You've got no right to—'

He stopped, because Wolf had now reached the little woodland shrine, and was arranging flowers and toys with a great self-absorbed sadness.

Wolf turned to Andrew as if they were in the midst of a companionable chat. 'There were those who didn't want us to put her here, in common ground,' he said. Andrew thought of the woman in the shop. 'But our little girl belongs near us.'

Andrew looked down at the home-made cross, and saw a name: *Jilly*. In his mind's eye he snatched the stick out of Wolf's hand and smashed it over the madman's head. Also in his mind's eye, the log turned out to be rotten, and broke harmlessly in two on contact with Wolf's impenetrable cranium.

IV. BING-BONG

Colleen's phone buzzed. She tapped the screen and said quietly, 'You speak. I listen.' She lay back on her pillows, rocking her spritzer in gentle circles so that the ice cubes clinked agreeably against the inside of the glass.

Gerry understood at once. (He always got her, just like that.) He spoke to her of the gentle play of light on water, the extraordinary kindness of the local people, this sort of Zen, compassionate calm that they had.

'You'd love it there, Colleen, you really would.'

'Mmm.' She lay back, propped on her pillow. She trailed her hand across her duvet, as if already watching it ebb and flow in the play of the gentle warm tide, stretching out a palm among the darting fishes, tiny and colourful, that swam right up to the beach.

'We're doing some wonderful work here too,' he was saying now. 'It's not just a haven for yogic ladies who lunch. Some of the breakthroughs that people are having – emotional, creative, even *spiritual* . . . Something really special is happening here. There's something almost *holy* about the atmosphere of the place!'

'Gerry the guru,' she teased in a whisper.

He laughed too, a warm, generous laugh that held nothing back and made you want to make him laugh again. 'It's happening to me too, Colleen! After years of feeling walled up, I feel as though I'm breaking through my shell, allowing my true self to emerge.'

'*Chrysalis*,' she whispered. It felt like kissing.

'Yes!' he whispered. 'This is a place of beginnings. Of fresh starts. Of things that are *coming to be.*'

She drifted off into a reverie. She and Gerry walking through the surf, hand in hand. She holding a group spellbound in a palm-fringed clearing by the Indian Ocean, helping wounded people to find their voices and walk tall again. She at dawn, sitting at a simple wooden table on a beach-side verandah, just Colleen and her laptop and the ocean, a cup of coffee and her challenging but exhilarating work-in-progress. She and Gerry, sarongs entwined . . .

A bing-bong sound roused her. She heard the muffled tones of a foreign voice speaking over a Tannoy.

'Gerry, where are you?'

V. THE FAMILIAR ACHE

What on earth did people do before box sets? Andrew asked himself with the sardonic weariness of a TV columnist who must bang out five hundred words about the final episode of an over-hyped series that he's barely watched.

There were certain series these days which he and Colleen felt obliged to say they had seen. Where once it might have been embarrassing to confess to a dinner-party crowd that you had never read *Jane Eyre* or *Hamlet* or *Lord of the* bloody *Rings* [there was a good scene about this in David Lodge somewhere], these days the same stigma of wordless but clearly sensed disapproval would be fixed on any couple who dared admit that they hadn't watched *Game of Thrones* or *The Wire* or *The Sopranos* or *Breaking Bad* or *Succession* [or whatever the latest craze was].

Mind you, when was the last time they had been to a dinner party?

Oh well, *tempora mutantur*, and all that. The times are changed, and we are changed with them. The conjugated form of *mutare* here a genuine passive, of course, not an indication of a deponent verb, as he had once misremembered. Deponent verbs being verbs that are passive in form but active in meaning, which Andrew thought summed up the exact opposite of his own case pretty well. He *looked* like he was capable of acting, he had legs, arms, eyes and a mind and everything. But he tended to be more on the receiving end of the verbing; not the agent but the *patient*. [Technically, then, he might best be described as a *concealed passive construction*.]

Andrew wondered if other people watched box sets the way he and Colleen did, i.e. they would put the thing on in the background, and then spend the evening scrolling through their phones or reading the paper with a glass of wine and a very occasional glance at *Better Call Saul* or *Line of Duty* till the regulation two-and-a-half episodes had been consumed, after which there was just time to tut a bit over *Question Time* or *Newsnight* before heading off to Bedfordshire. 'Watching box set X' could therefore be glossed more honestly as 'being in the same room while box set X was on'.

Of course, it was perfectly possible to read books in a similar way too. How else was anyone supposed to get through Faulkner or *Don Quixote*, or – dare one even whisper it – *Ulysses*? You hold up the page and your eyes sort of flutter over the words and sentences, but your mind never quite finds a foothold. [Since he was in the mood for literary

153

confessions, he supposed that now might be as good a time as any to admit that he had no real idea what a novella was.]

Andrew disapproved of Kindles but was a big fan of audio-books. He always got frustrated when people said to him things like: 'But can you really say you've read the book if you've only listened to it?' Well, he'd certainly read the book a damn sight more than someone who'd just seen a costume-drama adaptation. It always amazed him how many people claimed to have read *David Copperfield* who'd only seen some BBC version rather than, say, listened carefully to the thirty-four-hour unabridged recording by the sainted Martin Jarvis.

Audio was the only way to get through some books. *Moby-Dick* for example. But he *had* got through it, the whole fishy saga, so it was especially galling that time at the pub quiz when the tie-break question was 'What is the name of the ship in *Moby-Dick*?' and he couldn't for the life of him remember. But Tall-Paul knew, even though he hadn't read anything but *GQ* and *Men's Health* in decades. [And yes, he used the word *fishy* advisedly, since Melville himself describes the whale as a 'fish', not a mammal. As anyone would know who'd listened to the unabridged version, of course.]

So his mind ran on. Sitting on the opposite sofa to Colleen, he idly alternated between looking at his copy of *The Economist*, checking Twitter and even occasionally glanc-ing up at *The Good Wife*. Andrew always bought something worthy and momentous like *The Economist* when he went away. It was a holiday ritual of his, to flatter himself that he would read it cover to cover, and once again [*again?*] be fully up to speed with all the world's trends and tensions. Flicking through its austerely thin pages at WH Smith in the service station, he had happily imagined himself genning up on the latest expense scandal in Bulgaria, the burgeoning consti-tutional crisis in Guatemala, the rise of a new populist leader in Vietnam. Why, he might just read this every week, and be the well-informed, well-rounded world citizen he was always meant to be.

[In practice, he rarely got past the editorials.]

Colleen was flicking absently at her phone too. She was drinking fizzy water, which he took to mean she wasn't feeling too clever. She looked distantly beautiful, he couldn't help thinking, as if basking in the glow of a long-forgotten memory that had just returned to delight her anew. He looked at her graceful neck and her strong shoulders, felt the familiar ache return. [Unless of course it was a spritzer she was drinking; she was clever at disguising these, and in their world it wasn't done to challenge one another about such things.]

Neither of them had spoken for a good while; he couldn't even remember now how they had come to be watching *The Good Wife*, but the beauty of Netflix or whatever was that one episode just came on after another, requiring no debate or volition to keep the loop of the evening's entertainment rolling on.

Was their marriage on a loop too? He guessed that was up to Wolf now, really. Wolf who knew so much stuff about him that Andrew's mind reeled at the thought of trying to stem all his inadvertent leaks. He wouldn't know where to start, or stop.

What, in fact, did Wolf *not* know about him?

Andrew had almost enjoyed Ned's brief spell in prison. He had felt, or at least wanted to believe, that his son was safe in there. That controlled period of bed, board and supervision, he dared hope, would be a short sharp shock for Ned and a bit of respite care for an enabling parent. Accessory to a bodged burglary somewhere in Leeds, a first sentence; Ned was out in eight weeks. What Ned was doing up in Yorkshire was something he never explained. Ned told no one about his sentence, except of course his dad. It was a small thing amid the welter of the country's daily crime; there was no reason why Colleen should ever hear about it. Unless of course Wolf told her now.

Ned had not wanted his dad to visit him in jail, and he hadn't. But Andrew did go to the hospital after the amputation, which was first recommended by the prison doctor. It wasn't the whole foot, as Wolf implied, only a transmetatarsal excision of the left foot, as the surgeon described it. [*Only!*] Essentially they had sliced off the front half of the foot, so that in time he could even walk without crutches. Ned had been surprisingly stoical about the whole thing. *This is the op they make all the Arsenal players have,* he'd joked.

Andrew wept to see his son lose a part of himself. He blamed himself entirely, of course. He paid more guilt money to Ned, who took the cash but didn't seem to want him around to help. He was always on the move anyway.

Of course Andrew couldn't share any of the grief or the guilt with Colleen, and for months he lived in silent fear of her noticing a difference in his expressions, his moods, his behaviour. His not being himself [whatever that was]. It was a period where his and Colleen's boozing began to sync nicely, a period which, if he was honest, and emails from the Pauls notwithstanding, had continued pretty much up to the present.

He looked across again at Colleen, whose eyes were closed, one hand still clasping her phone and the other face up at the end of a bent arm, as if she had dozed off in the act of swearing an oath of allegiance. He wished for a moment that he could be her, or see her dreams, or perhaps just that he could kiss her again and find that she wanted to kiss him back. It was not the least of his sadnesses that throughout the whole of that dark post-amputation period, she had never apparently noticed a single thing that was different about him.

VI. PERSONAL BREAKTHROUGH

'Gerry, where are you?'

   'Where do you think?'

   'Er, Sri Lanka?'

   'Nope.'

   'Nope?'

   'Dubai. I'm on a transfer.'

   'Why?' But she knew.

   'I'm coming to get you.'

   Let me think. I'm not sure. Don't rush me.

He said, 'I need my life to start now, Colleen. That's *my* personal breakthrough. And I know now that my life is . . . well, *you.*'

   I don't even know if. The grandchildren. So much to . . . Andrew. Sonja. The twins. And . . . him. And now she thought she heard a small heart-breaking *miaow* at the back door.

There were so many things she should have said.

   But all she heard herself say was: 'Well, good luck finding the place.'

FRIDAY

Je sais que nous nous approchons peut-être de la fin de notre histoire. Je sais que je n'ose plus espérer une solution à notre crise. Mais sache au moins que je t'aimerai toujours. Si jamais tu a besoin de moi, tu n'auras que le dire.

Je ne souhaite pour toi que le bonheur et la paix. Je les souhaite pour nous deux, pourquoi pas. Je tiendrai toujours ton cœur dans mon cœur, pour pauvre récipient que ce soit. Et dans mes souvenirs je verrai toujours ton visage, lointain, exquis, souriant sa perfection.

[I know we are perhaps coming to the end of our story. I know that I no longer dare hope for a solution to our crisis. But know at least that I will always love you. If ever you need me, you just have to say so. I wish you – I wish us – only happiness and peace. I will always hold your heart in my own, paltry vessel though it be. And in my memories I will see always your lovely face from afar, smiling its perfection.]

I. A LITTLE SWAGGER

'So . . . who are you? And what is this?'

It was 8am. Andrew was standing next to Wolf by the open bonnet of their car, which Wolf had already begun working on and which still of course refused to start.

He was filled suddenly with a new determination to confront the scoundrel, to draw him out, to bring him to some sort of *justice* [while also trying to ensure in some way that Wolf didn't spill any of his secrets and ruin his entire life].

'Oh, I am the Walrus,' said Wolf instantly.

'Yeah. And I am the Eggman,' Andrew intoned back, in spite of himself. He was a big fan of late Beatles, and Wolf's familiarity with his playlists was almost a small comfort at this point, as well as being a sinister violation of course.

'Goo goo g'joob!' chorused Wolf delightedly. 'My dear boy, we are making music together!'

Andrew stared at the ground, his stars shining darkly over him. Wolf was a Hall of Mirrors, an endless onion, a riddle wrapped inside a mystery, an enigma of smoke and circumstance, all wrapped inside a really annoying pervy geriatric surveillance troll.

'I am the illegitimate son of the Beast of Jersey!' he was saying now. Jack was circling Andrew, getting in his way, doubling back and running round and confusing everything further. He was quite a chunky dog, Andrew noticed suddenly, with sharp teeth and an unquestioning fidelity to his mad owner. Wolf's wolf.

'Are you though?' asked Andrew.

'Not as such.'

'__'

Wolf bit into a piece of toast and began munching energetically. He made a noise and stuck a finger up as a sudden thought struck him. 'Or maybe . . . maybe you could think of me as a metaphor for Google, ja? A sort of living embodiment of the excesses of data, if you will.'

'You'd like that, wouldn't you?' said Andrew miserably. He had the sense of standing on ever-shifting sand once again. Sand that would slowly suck you down if you stood still for too long, like the sandy quagmire in the woods. Wolf's woods.

Blackmail was sort of game theory, wasn't it? And if it was a game, there had to be rules, no? And if there were rules, wasn't it just a matter of exploiting them to the disadvantage of your opponent?

Andrew had actually googled *game theory + blackmail*. There was some content there, but it all seemed rather complex. He looked at Wikipedia and Quora and various points in between. The material ranged from abstract theoretical papers to practical tips on taking the baddies down. At another time in his life – i.e. a time where he wasn't being urgently blackmailed – he would probably have found some of this stuff rather interesting. Then again, the material that wasn't complex wasn't really helpful either.

Stand up strong! Blackmailers are the scum of the earth.

Tell everyone your secrets – then the blackmailer has no power.

Stall the blackmailer – eventually your secrets won't matter so much any more. Like if they've got teenage pics of you, no one will care about these when you're thirty. (Unless you become a celeb.)

My cousin took vid of us doing it and now he says he send my mum

Thanks, internet. The power of the blackmailer lies in (a) the credibility of the incriminating material, and (b) your fear that exposure is a real risk, does it not? In theory, would this mean that the blackmailer's power is only potential? Well, true, perhaps . . . except that by revealing your secrets and robbing the blackmailer of their power over you, you will probably also ruin your own life, the fear of which is what gives the blackmailer their power in the first place. So much was obvious, no doubt, little more than a very roundabout re-statement of the phrase, *Help, I am being blackmailed!* But you had to be in the throes of being blackmailed yourself to fully appreciate what an exquisitely, fiendishly circular double-bind the whole thing was.

A certain idea struck him. What if he could blackmail Wolf back? What if he had something on his blackmailer?

'It's quite an unusual sort of hobby you've got,' said Andrew casually, imagining himself as a snake silently coiling and uncoiling around its hapless victim.

'What's that?' said Wolf, tinkering away.

'I mean, most men your age are playing golf, or building model railways, or . . .' His voice trailed away unconvincingly, as he realised he couldn't think of any more examples.

'Oh, yes! Well, each to his own, is what I say. I'm more interested in helping people out of their difficulties,' said Wolf, wiping his hands on an oily rag and staring lovingly at Andrew's engine.

'And your wife . . . Does she know about your penchant for spying on people?'

Wolf said nothing.

'And would you like her to know that we saw what you two get up to?'

Wolf turned pale. He dropped his spanner. 'Please, for the love of God . . . *She must never know what you saw*,' he whispered.

The tables were turning, just like that. Andrew walked away in the manner of a snake that has learned to swagger a little.

II. ACHIEVING THROUGH OTHERS

The strange thing about Gerry being on his way to rescue her from this week, this marriage, this life of hers – apart from the obvious unreality of the whole idea – was how it made Colleen suddenly *warm* to Andrew.

Now that she was apparently about to end things (?) with her husband of twenty years (and co-habiting partner for twenty-seven), Andrew started to appear to her – as he hadn't earlier that week (or much at all recently) – as a beacon of benevolent calm and good humour, a modest and unassuming man whom she knew wanted only good things for her and who clearly still wanted her *for her*, despite everything.

She looked at him now, quietly and patiently loading the dishwasher according to a method of his own devising, and it occurred to her that there was more of Wolf about him than she had given him credit for. Andrew got on with things, he cared about her, he tried hard to keep their show on the road in lots of unassuming but quietly important ways.

She looked at her watch: 11.17am. It was about a seven-hour flight from Dubai, she knew. Gerry might well be in the air now. Mind you, even when he landed, whenever that would be, it would probably take him, what, another two hours of faffing around to even get out of the airport. And then of course if he really was coming here, he was looking at several hours more of car or train. And that was just to reach the general vicinity; it had taken her and Andrew another couple of hours to negotiate the last five miles after that.

'Sorry, love. I need to take this.' She picked up her phone and walked out into the back garden, where she sat down on a bench in a rickety little wooden bower just out of view of the kitchen window.

Colleen's thoughts were interrupted by a rare call from Jav, one of her few gay clients. Quietly spoken and unassuming, Jav had originally been recommended to Colleen for help with projecting himself as a leader, after he was unexpectedly promoted to head of department and overnight became line manager to a bunch of people who used to be his colleagues.

It was an unenviable position; one day he was out getting drunk with his mates and bitching about the boss – and then the next day, he *was* the boss. Jav had to deal with other people's resentment of his new position, and find a way of getting his former co-workers to understand that they were now accountable to him. So Colleen and Jav had sketched out a rough programme of areas to look at, such as assertiveness, balancing personal and professional relationships, learning to delegate and *achieve through others*, handling difficult conversations, and so on. But of course, after a couple of chats, that thing happened again, and Colleen found herself rapidly promoted once more from corporate trainer to unofficial life coach, sounding board, shoulder-to-cry-on and spiritual guru – and all on the company's ludicrously well-paid time, of course.

As his private listener, Colleen discovered that Jav's big secret was his relationship with Eric, a French broker who worked for the same firm. It was a highly traditional place, where intimate relationships between co-workers were frowned upon and, incredibly, same-sex relationships still remained unmentionable. Worse still, Jav was now actually Eric's line manager, which was officially prohibited. The whole thing had to be kept under wraps.

The change in their working dynamic had not been easy, and for months Jav had been telling Colleen tearful tales of Eric's growing indifference to him. Jav suspected that Eric was seeing someone else at their work, or at least dallying with the idea. He suspected the culprit was a woman, which was especially upsetting because, although Eric had been out with women before, he'd always said Jav had helped him to embrace his true identity, as a gay man. So this affair, if true, was like a double betrayal. (Although in Colleen's experience, most people found a way to frame their betrayal as double these days, one way or another. It was like the way menu portions and chocolate bars were always getting bigger: everyone had to have their portion of pain supersized.)

'Colleen! It's Jav!'

'Hello, you!' said Colleen, with practised delight. 'You sound really well!'

'I am,' said Jav. 'I mean, we are!'

'Ooh! Do tell.' As she listened, she was aware of a small presence landing silently by her. It was her little friend, rolling over and arching his back, shamelessly showing off his white tummy fluff. Smiling, she reached out a hand and tickled him gently.

Jav – whom Colleen herself would have divorced years ago for his total lack of a self-edit button – now related in excruciating detail the massive row he'd had with Eric on Tuesday night, *no, wait, the Wednesday*. They were supposed to be going out for an anniversary dinner – *you know that new Japanese place on the Strand, the one with the giant griddle thing and the beautiful one-way glass screens that change colour and look like a waterfall when you walk past on the street, but inside they're completely transparent? It's had the most amazing reviews – they even have that special fish flown in that's supposed to be like the most amazing delicacy in the world but it's poisonous if you do it wrong and the chef needs a special licence to be allowed to cook it, you know? So anyway, we looked at all the comments online and we were both gonna go for the tempura salmon starters that come with this amazing sauce that apparently looks like gravy but is actually made from the ink of this squid that only lives in one part of the South China Sea but then . . .*

And so on and on. The long and short of it all was that Eric had cancelled their dinner date at the last minute. Jav was furious, and terrified, so he went home . . . where he found his partner curled up in a ball crying. And that's when it all came out. Eric had been hearing voices. Not hostile ones, but scary nonetheless. So he'd been to see someone in secret and had been diagnosed with an anxiety disorder and prescribed some drugs. He was terrified of telling Jav because he thought Jav wouldn't want to be lumbered with a mad person. They had it all out, and Jav was able to reassure Eric, and now they were working through it all together. They had never felt closer! And Colleen was a big part of it.

'I did that exercise of yours with him, you know the one where you each write down your ideal timeline over the next month, next year, next five years?' said Jav. 'Remember?'

'Oh, yes,' said Colleen nervously. She reached out to stroke the cat again, but now her hand hovered uncertainly in mid-air. The cat sprang to its feet, suddenly suspicious and vigilant.

'Yeah. And when we each compared timelines, we saw that we wanted the same things, and we wanted a future full of each other! *And our kids!* And once we'd worked that out, it was just a matter of thinking what we need to do to get there.'

Colleen, who had been expecting another relentless stream of bitter paranoia, found that her voice was all wobbly.

'That's wonderful, Jav. I'm so happy for you both.' The cat was back, she was stroking him under the chin, and he was rubbing his cheeks against her and purring. She made a point of focusing on her call, and not looking at the cat directly. Not making a *thing* of this new intimacy.

'Of course, if I'd known what Eric was going through, I'd have sent him to you,' said Jav. 'But he found this expert on his own. Some sort of . . . consultant psychologist?'

Colleen coughed. 'So you both had your bit on the side, so to speak.'

Jav laughed, and Colleen laughed. They talked a little about mental health, and how it was something that affected everyone sooner or later – and what was that stat about three in five people hearing voices at some stage in their life (or was that rats in London?) – and how it was time to end the stigma and speak out. Though he and Eric wouldn't be doing this at their own work just yet, as the three people who'd signed up for their work's newly formed Wellbeing Council had since been made redundant, apparently for completely unrelated reasons, but still.

The call ended with general agreement that there was still a long way to go. But Jav and Eric were in a great place, at least, and none of it could have happened without Colleen.

'Thank you SO much, Colleen,' said Jav. 'Oh God, I shouldn't really but I have to tell someone my secret.'

'Oh? No, no, it's OK. You don't have to,' said Colleen, feeling she was probably sorted already on the secrets front.

'We're *engaged!*'

At this Colleen came over all wobbly again. 'That's wonderful!' she said, almost unable to speak. 'Now you just . . .' She stifled a sob.

'Colleen?'

'You just be kind to each other.'

She sat caressing the little cat's perfect head for a few quiet minutes. She went to fetch him some more tuna, but when she returned, he had vanished again.

She stood by the fence where she had first seen him and called, but he was gone, and for an awful moment she was utterly alone again, alone with the grey weary sadness that comes with losing everything.

III. A BLUEPRINT FOR THE FUTURE

Andrew had played his cards, and played them well, to immediate gratifying effect. Only, as he realised now, he had no idea what happened next.

An obvious problem was that Wolf still knew all the things that he knew. Andrew had no way of knowing if he was still gathering data either. Could he at least rely now on Wolf to keep his mouth shut? It wasn't as if Wolf was ever going to sign anything to that effect. [And if he did, he'd probably insist on putting his name on the side of a mackerel or a cow, like people used to do with charity cheques in the old days. And even then, his word probably wouldn't be worth the heifer it was daubed on.]

Did Andrew need to actually deliver on his threat, he wondered, or at least pretend to, in order for Wolf to take him seriously? He was a notoriously timid and non-confrontational man, as Wolf had doubtless realised. In any case, Wolf was, by his own estimation, either a walrus or a metaphor for big tech, which was to say he was completely fruitloops, and therefore utterly unpredictable.

Colleen, meanwhile, had apparently decided that Wolf and Hildy offered some sort of blueprint for a long and happy marriage. This baffled Andrew in one way, but also made him cautiously optimistic, since Colleen seemed to be hinting that here was a model for them to follow. The idea that they had any sort of way forward was very cheering. [He'd been working on a farewell message to her recently, in French of course, which even he could see was hopelessly, mawkishly, pleased with itself.]

'They are quite the devoted couple, in their own way,' she was saying now, looking out the window at Wolf pushing Hildy round the garden. She and Andrew were picking their way through a lunch of *bits and bobs*, their long-standing term for any meal improvised from leftovers that needed using up as, typically, at the end of a holiday. It wasn't a bad meal in its way: lettuce, tomatoes, cucumber, feta cheese. Some pine nuts, cottage cheese. A bowl of tuna mayonnaise. Some ham. Some slices of pizza, another dish that was, to his mind, best served cold.

'Here, you've got a bit of cottage cheese on your lip.' Colleen leaned across and brushed the offending morsel away from his mouth. It was a surprisingly intimate thing, especially as she quietly mimed a kiss as she did so.

'Yes,' she was saying now. 'We could all learn a thing or two from the Wolfs.'

167

'Like about snooping, you mean,' said Andrew, but his heart wasn't really in it. Colleen was looking fondly at the cross-word now, inviting him to move next to her on the kitchen bench and partake with her in the holy sacrament of cryptic clue-solving.

O time, thou must untangle this, not I. It is too hard a knot for me to untie!

He slid over, and snuggled into her warmth. All in all, it had been quite a week. They'd done a lot of crosswords when they were courting.

IV. SPOILT FOR CHOICE

As it was Friday at last, the last full day of their stay, Colleen walked over to the big house with a bottle of red and the urge to have one last chat with Hildy.

Wolf ushered her in. Mrs Wolf was 'temporarily indis-posed', he said, but she was very welcome to come in and wait. Taking him up on his offer of a cup of coffee, Colleen followed Wolf into the kitchen at the back of the house.

'We've had a lovely week,' said Colleen idly, as Wolf busied himself with a cafetière and a special cone-shaped brown plastic spoon that was obviously reserved for doling out precise measures of ground coffee. 'It's been such a pleasure to meet you both and get to know you . . . a little.'

'Oh, the pleasure has been all ours, dear lady!' Wolf shot back. 'Oh yes, we've enjoyed having you here *very much.* I'm just sorry that you haven't been able to get around as much as you'd have wanted to. Hopefully Tony will be back with that part this afternoon.'

'Oh, not to worry, not to worry at all!' returned Colleen. 'Not being able to move has given us a nice . . . break from things,' she said. There was a slightly awkward pause, as if each was considering the plausibility of her last remark from their respective angles, and perhaps wondering if it was entirely well-chosen, considering that poor old Hildy was in a chair most of the time, so would never know the luxury of taking a break from getting around as much as you want.

'You really have such charming grandchildren,' said Wolf, moving them onto safer ground.

'Thank you!' said Colleen enthusiastically. 'They're . . . they really are the light of our lives.' Clearly, her powers of small talk were fading fast. Well, it had been a long week.

'Yes, yes. I can quite see.' Wolf looked thoughtful. 'I have no children to come see me,' he said simply. It was an odd, sad way of putting it. She must go and look at that grave before they left.

'Oh, I'm so sorry. Did you and Hildy—'

'She has none either.'

Colleen didn't quite know how to take this. Perhaps he thought she was asking if they'd been married before. To other people? But it was clear that the topic was now closed, just as abruptly as Wolf had opened it. There was another pause in the conversation now, almost but not quite devoid of awkwardness.

'She'll be along very soon,' said Wolf with another sooth-ing change of topic. 'She is very particular about her *toilette*, as you can imagine,' he said. 'It's one of the few things she can still have control over. It doesn't do to rush her.' He brushed an imaginary speck of dust from the back of an armchair.

'I think . . .' Colleen paused. She felt strangely weepy and weak again. 'I want you to know . . .' she essayed at last, once she was more confident that her voice wasn't about to give way. 'I want you to know that I think the way you look after your wife is absolutely inspirational,' she got out at last.

'My wife?' said Wolf, arching an eyebrow.

'Oh,' said Colleen.

'Hildy! My wife?' Wolf snorted with delight. He looked about him rapidly, as if desperate to share the joke with Hildy at once. Or anyone.

'I'm so sorry,' said Colleen, baffled. Perhaps Wolf was . . . her boyfriend? Perhaps they were a new couple? She was embarrassed at her conventional thinking. Just because they were an older couple, that didn't mean they had to be married, did it? Or that they'd been together for, like, fifty years? Perhaps they were . . . companions?

'Oh, my dear, no!' Wolf spluttered. 'Hildy isn't my wife!'

'I'm so sorry,' began Colleen. 'I'm so sorry, I just assumed . . .' But wait. Hadn't he himself referred to Hildy as 'Mrs Wolf'?

'She's my sister!'

'Then why would you let her beat you with a strap?' It was Andrew who was asking, Andrew who had appeared unheard at the kitchen door.

'Ahh!' Wolf put down his coffee and arched another delighted eyebrow, this time in Andrew's direction. He was almost camp at such moments.

'Why?' repeated Andrew. There was an uncharacteristic steeliness to his voice. Colleen liked it.

'Wolffffffff! I'm coming down!' Hildy squawked from some-where upstairs.

He looked to the ceiling. 'Righty-ho, dear!' he called back. Then he turned to Andrew.

'Oh,' sighed Wolf, looking suddenly sheepish. 'You saw that.'

'Yes. You know I did.'

'Well, Hildy was . . . cross with me. With good reason.'

'Also, there's no such car part as a transponder.'

'Oh?'

'Though you do get them in listening devices, things like that.'

Wolf tried to stammer something, looked flustered, and Colleen's heart went out to him. 'I'm not very good with the names of things,' he said helplessly.

'Well, I'm phoning the AA!' said Andrew and stormed out. Goodness, but he was being decisive all of a sudden. In the background, Colleen heard a smooth whirring sound.

'But your membership's expired – I checked!' Wolf called after him. 'Please excuse me, ladies,' he said to Colleen with great courtesy. 'I have your husband upset. I must make amends.' He bustled out after Andrew.

'Oh, dear me,' said Hildy, who had descended in her stair-lift and was now walking laboriously with two sticks across to a wheelchair. Colleen went to help her into it, but Hildy shooed her away.

'I'm sorry about Andrew,' said Colleen. 'He's quite on edge – what with the car and everything.'

Hildy nodded sagely. 'I know, dear,' she said. 'It's been a difficult week for the pair of you.'

'Yes.'

'Still, at least you got some, eh?' she chortled delightedly. She reminded Colleen once again of Nursey in the Tudor *Blackadder*.

'I . . .'

'And of course you'll be spoilt for choice soon, won't you, you saucy little tart?'

'Err . . .'

'Mmm,' continued Hildy. 'But whose car will you be going back in, I wonder? Which boy racer will you be parking in your hot love-garage tonight?'

'My love-garage.' Colleen could only repeat things.

'Andrew . . . ?'

'*Andrew*,' said Colleen, mesmerised. Hildy leaned in closer, so that Colleen could make out the tiny red veins etched in the older woman's cheeks and nose that lay under a dusty patina of crudely applied foundation. Colleen thought suddenly of the surface of Mars.

'Or that naughty Gerry?'

V. THE TIP OF THE TIP OF THE ICEBERG

A couple of hours later Andrew was putting his boxers back on, a post-coital habit of his, having made love with his wife for only the second time in just over twelve weeks – the first, if you counted the times he actually remembered.

Not that he'd been counting, he said. Not that it mattered if he had, she said.

They lay there in cosy quiet proximity staring at different things in their holiday bedroom, examining bedside knick-knacks and reading out choicely brutal lines from stories of mass murderers and human cannibals, until Colleen picked up the crossword again.

'T-R-E-A-C-H-E-R-Y,' she said with triumph.

'That's a bit harsh,' bantered Andrew, though he was suddenly anxious. 'I did my best.'

She laughed. 'No, look!' she said. 'Fifteen down.'

Really extreme instructor breeds the worst kind of infidelity (9)

'Oh yes!' he said. 'The extremes of *really* — R and Y — plus *instructor* = teacher. Teacher + RY = T-R-E-A-C-H-E-R-Y.' He wrote the answer in with a red biro, the only pen to hand, and they high-fived contentedly. Just like the old days.

'Here, this one looks vulnerable,' said Colleen now. 'Ten letters, second one H, last two T-H.' A *vulnerable* clue was one which in their private lingo was ripe to yield its secret, usually because they had several letters for it or because an especially pregnant element had been revealed, such as a rare O at the end of the word, or a Z as second letter.

Shh to Bible? Not everyone can say that. (10)

'It looks like an anagram,' mused Colleen, sucking the end of her pen.

'Don't put that in your mouth,' Andrew snapped suddenly. 'You don't know where it's been.' He made an impatient nudging sound, the sort of sound made by someone who has been played, yet again.

'It's OK, love, you can't help being better at these than me.'

'It's not that, it's . . .' He stopped.

'Come on, spit it out! You solve the clue and then I try to work out why, that's always been our way.'

'S-H-I-B-B-O-L-E-T-H,' he said, very softly. He felt weak and treacherous and broken.

'Oh yes!' she said, writing it in. 'What does that mean again?'

Shibboleth was one of his very favourite words. Helplessly he mansplained to her about the Gileadites and the Ephraimites, and *lollapalooza*, and the Parsley Massacre, and the way 'fish and chips' can be used to tell Kiwi and Aussie English speakers apart.

Colleen seemed interested, at least at first. But he was a dreadful completist in his explanations, and he sensed he was losing her. He was losing himself, to be honest. The appearance of that word, as per Wolf's prediction, reminded him oddly of Peter's denial of Christ three times before the cock crowed. [And incidentally, was that story the source of 'the chickens coming home to roost' in some way? One to look up.]

Though not a believer, Andrew had always thought the Passion a magnificent story. And he had always thought the words, *And Peter went outside and wept bitterly*, to be among the most poignant in the whole Bible. [Peter was generally the most poignant character in the whole saga too, he always thought. That bit where he tries to walk on the water always got him.] *Of course* Peter would swear that he'd never deny Christ, and no doubt he truly meant it at the time, just as

Andrew had sworn not to say *Shibboleth*, sworn not to enable Ned. And of course when push came to shove, Peter, like Andrew, would let himself down completely. Because he was only a man, after all, making impossible promises to an impossible God.

[Of course he ought to have been crosser about his phone being hacked than about someone tampering with his cryptic crossword. But – and he sensed obscurely that this went somewhere near the heart of what was wrong with him – he really wasn't.]

In the bedroom there was a pause now, a sudden atmosphere that was more than just the overspill of Andrew being boring. He tensed. The moment had become pregnant.

'Andrew,' she said.

Oh God. 'Yes, love.' His urge was to assume the foetal position.

'I know about Ned, you know.'

He froze for an instant, put the paper down and sat back on his propped-up pillow.

'Ned?' he said, stalling helplessly.

'You know,' she said, not unkindly. 'The joint at Tom and Maura's.'

'The joint at Tom and Maura's?'

'You know.'

Oh God, *the joint at Tom and Maura's*! There had been a time in his life when Andrew had been racked with guilt about the joint at Tom and Maura's. The joint he had let Ned have a few puffs of when he was only fourteen and they were at this end-of-year barbecue in the garden of one of the families from school, and no one else was around and he was a bit pissed and was trying to bond with his recalcitrant teenage son. Showing off. Playing the man of the world. Currying favour. Trying to be less cringe, to regain a tiny bit of cred.

Go on then, Ned, just a puff and a sip. And don't tell your mum.

Later on, when they did therapy and counselling and all the rest, Ned was sometimes asked if there was a trigger moment that had first got him interested in drugs. At such times Andrew always thought guiltily of the joint at Tom and Maura's which was, as far as he knew, Ned's first encounter with drugs or alcohol. [Though what did he know really?] It was utterly his fault that it had happened, but Ned never mentioned it. He never knew whether Ned was protecting him, or whether it wasn't really significant in the scheme of things, and of course Andrew was too guilty to ever ask.

Plus, coward that he was, if Ned had forgotten about it, Andrew wasn't about to bring the moment back to his or *other people's* attention.

The only reason Andrew wasn't racked with guilt about the joint at Tom and Maura's any more was that his mental shame-drive was so full of more recent and far more heinous offences relating to Ned that he simply didn't have the processing memory to hold it all.

He said, 'I'm so sorry.' A remnant of the scene played itself in his mind. Him and Ned sitting on the edge of a trampoline, a litter of continental lager bottles, an abandoned Swingball set. Laughter from the patio. Some urban choon that the kids liked, booming out through the French windows.

'I know.'

'How did you know?'

'Ned told me.'

'When?'

'About seven years ago.'

Oh God. 'And you've known that all this time?'

'Yes.'

'That's not like you.' She gave him a sharp look, until he added hastily, 'Not to say something, I mean. You always say, "Better out than in".'

175

'I've been trying to forgive you,' she said.

'All this time?'

'Yes. Well, and no, for lots of it.'

Andrew's voice trembled. There was a time when Colleen's forgiveness was all that he craved. But there was so much more that she didn't even know about. This was not even the tip of the tip of the iceberg of the forgiveness that he would require, and his mind swooned at the precipice.

'Every time we make love,' he said instead, 'I always fear it will be the last.' It sounded like a non sequitur, but they both knew it wasn't.

Colleen kissed him tenderly but said nothing. She picked up her phone and slipped out of the room.

VI. THE TRUTH FARM

In the great expanse of time between Friday lunch and dinner, Colleen found Wolf in the garden. He was down on his haunches, hands dirty and forehead shiny, doing something timeless with the cabbages.

'It's time,' she said.

He stood and looked at her levelly, wiping the soil from his hands.

'Yes,' he said. 'You have had honesty thrust upon you. You have the right to some honesty from me.'

'How could I ever trust anything you ever say?'

'Oh, touché!' Wolf giggled. 'It's been quite a ride, has it not?'

Colleen stared at him.

'How did you know about Gerry?' she asked at last.

'Oh, simple things. You know, phones and networks.'

'You spied on us.'

'And mics. Cameras.'

'Cameras?'

Wolf led her into the shed, where he sat Colleen down on his leather swivel chair, gave her some headphones, and

176

played a sort of highlights reel of the week. She watched Andrew stash his stupid bottles in the stupid peg bag. Andrew, half-cut, banging himself on the car boot. Andrew falling into the rockery. Sonja sneaking a late-night joint.

Colleen saw herself in the garden, speaking quietly but flirtatiously into her phone, the smile on her face the smile of a person she didn't recognise.

She saw Andrew dodging a hail of missiles, thrown pretty randomly by someone who looked like her. Now she saw herself and Andrew. It was all a bit grainy, and black and white, but it intrigued her, despite everything.

Wolf clicked the file shut, and exhaled solemnly, as if he had just delivered himself of a painful but necessary charge sheet. He didn't look as though he expected her to launch herself at him, or spit in his face, or start screaming abuse. These were all ways she should have reacted, she knew, and yet – and as Wolf seemed to have anticipated – she did nothing. She was aware only of a feeling of extraordinary icy calm.

'I knew it.'

The videos were an appalling violation, but that was just something people said. If the worst violation you experienced in your life was someone filming you in the shower, you should probably count yourself lucky. Perhaps it was the actress in her; she had invaded her own privacy often enough in the old days. She wasn't even really surprised by her own reaction, just as for some reason she hadn't been very surprised that her first impulse on discovering that Hildy (and Wolf) knew she was plotting to leave her husband (sort of) was . . . to make love with her husband.

'Wow,' she said. 'You are quite the little Peeping Tom.'

'It's just a . . . Just something I do,' said Wolf modestly. 'A hobby, if you will.'

Colleen smiled sarcastically. 'So, let me see if I've got this. You hire out your cottage as a holiday home, and then spy on the occupants. And this is, what? How you get your rocks off?'

'Well. Let's just say that it's interesting to see how people behave when placed under certain . . . pressures.'

'I see. So we are a sort of experiment for you?'

'We hold up a mirror to people. The world is a dangerous place, I don't have to tell you that. I show people their shadow side, get them to think about what really matters to them. I find out a little about them, so that I can offer some gentle help. But of course, it's all done in a controlled environment.'

'Oh, that's all right then,' said Colleen. 'But shouldn't you maybe give people a bit of warning? I don't seem to remember signing a waiver when we booked?'

'A waiver?'

'You know, the sort of thing people used to have to sign before they went on the *Jerry Springer Show*.'

'Well, of course, there's nothing explicit about all this beforehand,' said Wolf good-naturedly, as if dealing with a perfectly reasonable but easily addressed objection, one he had heard many times before. 'But if you knew exactly what was coming, the whole exercise wouldn't work, would it?'

'Perhaps *you* should go and work for Gerry.'

'Perhaps I should. But of course I am needed here.'

'Your wife . . . Does she know you do all this? I mean, your sister?' For all Colleen knew, Wolf had lied about being married to Hildy rather than being her brother. Come to that, with Wolf it might even be that Hildy was his wife *and* his sister.

Wolf ignored her question. 'I see it actually as a sort of public service we're running here,' he said. 'We're thinking of calling it . . . *The Truth Farm*. What do you think?'

'Words . . . fail me,' said Colleen.

'Now there's a first.'

'Wait. Did you say *We?*'

Wolf smiled. 'I did indeed, fair lady.' He wore the patient, good-natured smile of a teacher with a backward student for whom the penny has finally, finally dropped.

'You mean, Hildy knows about . . . all of this?'

'My dear Colleen.' He laughed sadly, with a slow sweep of his hand at all his screens and headphones and tangles of wire. 'Hildy is *the reason* I do all this.'

VII. A SELFISH SILO

Andrew was back in the meadow, doing steps. It was a thing he did, whenever there was too much conflict or stress for him to handle.

It was like when they were at home, and they were in the middle of an argument, and Andrew would start doing manic amounts of housework in order to defuse the tension. He would empty the dishwasher, put clothes away, mow the lawn, scrub the downstairs loo . . . He was so efficient, in fact, that Colleen liked to joke that it was in her interest to provoke even more fights because it kept the house so tidy.

Andrew hated being in mid-argument with Colleen. He hated the suspension of cordialities, the absence of smiles, the withdrawal of warmth. The sense of exile from the sunny side of the street. He hated his habit of continuing the row with other people, when she wasn't even around. They weren't in that tense place now, of course, quite the opposite. But he had the feeling that this was only a temporary stay of execution.

Colleen always seemed so alive to him, more alive than he had ever felt himself. She was brave, she burned with passion, she threw herself into things [she threw things, admittedly], she was endlessly interested in other people and the external world. He had always imagined himself as a sneaky parasite, secretly trying to siphon off some of that energy to top up his own meagre store. He had never managed to express to her what she meant to him. She was clever and wise and funny; over the years his desire for her had never dimmed. But perhaps he couldn't say what she meant to him because he feared there was something fundamentally self-serving about his love for her.

Colleen had saved him from himself. Moved by his own passion for her, he had made audacious declarations and undertaken romantic stunts of all kinds. Inspired by her faith in him, he had pushed himself forward for work, said no to unreasonable clients, confronted difficult relatives. Spurred on by her example, he had tried to be more pro-active, assertive, even bold. Not much to shout about, by other people's standards, no doubt, but much more than he would have been otherwise. It seemed impossible to avoid clichés, but perhaps that didn't matter if you could inhabit the hoary words to the extent that someone believed you meant them.

So say it then: Colleen made him want to be a better person. She made him want to be someone else.

He wanted to keep her for himself, of course, tuck them both away in a selfish silo where no one else could reach them. This was a ludicrous ambition, he knew, because Colleen's whole being was pointed at the Other, at the External, and it was only his passive solipsism that made him think any other outlook was remotely normal or acceptable. He shuddered at the thought of all the contortions that Colleen must have had to put her personality through in order to survive living with him – a man who'd rather stay in than go out, who preferred dead people to live ones, who'd rather read about life than experience it, whose default response to any new opportunity or idea was a suspicious No.

She was the sun. And he wasn't even the moon.

VIII. WALKING IN SPACE

Early that Friday evening, Colleen and Andrew ate the home-made lasagne that Hildy had made for them as part of their welcome pack. It had sat forgotten in the freezer all week, until Andrew, performing some of his pre-packing house-clearing rituals, had unearthed it the previous night. They sat at right angles to each other on one corner of the kitchen bench. The crossword lay face up between them, though neither seemed very committed to solving any clues.

Both of them, Colleen noticed, had tucked their phones away from view. She was gasping for a glass of red, but she wasn't sure if the fragile peace that seemed to be reigning between them would be able to cope with such a move.

'You were right about Wolf all along,' she said at last.

'Yes,' he said. 'Though I still don't really know why he does it all.'

'*They*,' she corrected.

'*They*,' he agreed, shaking his head. 'Do you think they really are brother and sister?'

'Kissing cousins, more like,' she said. It was an attempt at humour, but neither of them laughed. They were, she decided, in an oddly humourless place just then.

Colleen leaned across and stroked the side of Andrew's face. He leant his cheek into her gratefully. She imagined there was so much to say, so much for both of them to hear, and yet stringing words together had never seemed harder. She thought of wading through treacle, and old recordings that go funny when the tape gets chewed.

'I'm going to go out for a bit,' she said.

'Of course.' Andrew nodded manically, as if this was exactly what he expected her to do. He began busying himself with the plates and the dishwasher.

She picked up her phone and her handbag, and headed out across the gravel in the direction of the meadow until she was out of sight of their kitchen. Andrew, she knew, was tracking her path with a dumb Jack-like gaze.

The prospect of Gerry arriving here of all places remained an idea whose reality she still fundamentally doubted. She kept expecting him to text and say he'd been joking, or that he'd changed his mind and turned around at Frankfurt or Istanbul, or that he'd just remembered that he was only a figment of her fantasy life so wouldn't be able to come in person.

Wolf knew about Gerry, of course, and she knew she should be worried that he'd tell Andrew. But Wolf seemed to her even less real than Gerry, about as plausible a character as Sir Andrew Aguecheek. Plus, Wolf's ways were so complex and devious that just blurting out what he knew seemed far too crass and obvious a move for him. No fun; not really in his line at all.

Hildy knew about Gerry too, she suddenly recalled, and this was rather more troubling, because Hildy was a personage so preposterous that she made Wolf and Gerry (and Sir Andrew Aguecheek) seem utterly credible, even humdrum. As Colleen wandered around the perimeter of the meadow, she caught sight of a light peeping out from around the other side of the big house.

Wolf was in his lair once more. She stubbed out her Silk Cut, and headed for his shed.

SATURDAY

*I was alone in those days. I lived alone, worked alone, drank
alone. The war was over, but memories lingered. People weren't
ready to forget – or forgive. No place for the likes of me in a
land like this. I could never fit in. I'd had a couple of friends at
school, till the others scared them out of it. I was good at football
and I could do the work all right. But my step-parents were the
sort who kept themselves to themselves. They were simple folk
who worked the land and distrusted visitors. When it came to
the time of girls and girlfriends . . . well, I was never much good
at that. Girls scared me. They were bright gaudy things, full of
wild colours and unpredictable energies and challenging
laughter. They made me feel things I didn't understand and
didn't know how to control. I kept away from them as much as I
could. At night, dreams of my sister haunted me.*

*She saved me from all that, in the end. When I got her back,
she had changed. But she needed me, and I needed that. Now
we won't be parted, not now, not ever.*

I. DOGS ON STRING

Saturday. Colleen, who had been up half the night, started
from another fitful doze, and found herself thinking about
her son. It was still disappointingly early.

Thinking about Ned was not something she allowed
herself to do as a rule, but she was on holiday and a bit out of

sorts, so the banned thoughts and feelings were able to slip in unchallenged. And anyway: all that was before last night.

The last time she had seen Ned, a lifetime ago, they had driven side by side to a hostel place they knew, where she had dropped him off. Ned looked straight ahead, registering neither protest nor approval of the situation. In silence they had gone round to the boot of the car. There had been an awkward moment as both had gone to get the rucksack out at the same time.

Ned stood on the pavement, meek but impatient, as if waiting to be dismissed. The only words that came to Colleen were the dead clichés of parenting.

'We're just trying to help, the best way we can.' She had a nasty feeling that she even said, 'You'll thank us for this one day.' *Jesus wept.*

'Yeah.' He shuffled on the spot, looking at his feet. In their lives at home they had seen him as a powerful anarchic force, a bigger, badder version of the hyper-boisterous little boy that had once blown through their lives. Even in his addiction, she had drawn a secret comfort from his energy, his larger-than-life spirit – just as when he was a little boy, she used to secretly applaud his audacity even when she was in the middle of giving him a public telling-off.

But now, suddenly, he looked small and frail and forlorn, her little lad cut adrift in a world of pitiless men and women, whose currency was violence and despair. She gave Ned an envelope with £500 in it. She knew it probably wouldn't last him more than twenty-four hours. In his eyes that wouldn't meet hers, there was no reproach, no criticism, no defiance. Worse than that, far worse: there was nothing.

He was forever upending their lives, tearing their comfortable existence apart. But as she drove away, tears streaming down her face, gulping back the snot, hiccupping with grief, she knew already that the only thing worse than him causing all that mayhem was him *not* doing so. Him not being around.

Until now she had always thought at least she knew who to blame. Until now, she had managed to block out the worst of her fears about what might be happening to him. It was for the best. There was no other way. This was tough love.

Imagine, she had always wanted to say to Andrew. *Imagine loving someone so much that genuinely the best thing you can think to do for them is to slam the door in their face? Kick them out in the street? Throw them to the wolves?*

But she didn't say these things. If he saw her give an inch, she knew he'd crack open completely. For all she knew, he'd secretly been helping Ned anyway; she was pretty sure that Sonja had. And secretly, on one level, she didn't mind; if it kept her son alive, she was very, very glad. But on the level that had to count, she violently resented having to be strong for both of them. Especially when it took everything just to be strong for herself.

And then last night had happened, and it was she who had cracked wide open.

II. BREAKDOWN ASSISTANCE

'Our love is like . . .'

'Let me stop you there,' she said.

Saturday morning, 10.30am. They were drinking coffee at the little table in the garden. It was a lovely suntrap at this hour, and it was a shame that they had only discovered this now, on the very brink of their departure.

Colleen's eyes, he noticed, looked dry and red. He had no idea what time she came to bed. But there was also a strangely settled calmness about her, as if she had finally made peace with a difficult truth, or taken a painful but necessary decision.

'I was going to say our love is like . . . the winter sun.'

'Go on. Let's hear it.'

'Past its zenith but blazing still. A warm glow in a low sky.'

'It's dazzling on those rare occasions when it actually appears.'

'Yes!' he said, encouraged.

'No,' she said firmly. 'I mean it's literally blinding. It makes driving a total nightmare.'

'"*I hate your logic like I hate an empty wine goblet*",' he quoted.

'And even when it hits you, it doesn't even keep you warm,' she persisted, driving in a final nail. 'It sort of creates coldness around itself.'

'Wow,' said Andrew. 'You really know how to slaughter a metaphor.'

'Sorry,' she said. 'It's a gift I have. Or a curse.'

'Correction!' he said. 'I think, anyway. It's probably not so much a metaphor, and more of an analo—'

He stopped because she was looking at him, almost fondly, because he was doing it again, he knew he was. 'We all have them, don't we?' she said.

'What?'

'Our funny little ways.'

'Sorry.'

She looked out at the familiar yellow van, which she imagined muttering soothing words and transferring vital life-energy to their crappy old Astra, under the calm super-vision of an engineer in a hi-viz jacket.

'That van's got a big AA on the side of it,' she said at last. 'Do you think it's trying to tell us something?'

He looked at their cardboard box of empties and sighed. 'Very probably.'

He added: 'It also says something on there about break-down assistance.'

'Relationship breakdown?' She smiled sadly. 'Let's not ask for miracles.'

'OK.'

A dog barked, a dog they knew well.

'Oh God.'

'What?'

'The grave. I've just realised.'

'Yes?'

'You said you saw the name Jilly on it?'

'Yes.'

'*Jack and Jill went up the hill . . .*'

'Stop it.'

'It's a dog's grave.'

'Oh, for God's sake.'

'Jack's sister, no doubt.'

'Jack's twin.'

They couldn't help laughing, or trying to. What else was there to do now? But it was a willed, defeated sort of laughter, and it soon fizzled out. Perhaps, she thought. Perhaps if they hadn't been hungover or half-cut or feuding all week – or if she hadn't been daydreaming about Gerry (a no-show, thank God) – they might have noticed sooner what was going on. Silence soon weighed in on them again. Perhaps some good would come of all this, but it was a horrible, flat, squalid feeling, to have been so comprehensively mocked and manipulated.

'Madam,' said Andrew, reading her thoughts. 'We have been *most notoriously abused.*'

'You can bloody say that again, Malvolio.'

'I'm sorry.'

'But anyway!' she said briskly. 'We're going to see Ned. It's time.'

'Yes?' he said, looking her square in the eyes.

'Yes,' she said, looking squarely back. 'We'll always have Ned.'

He nodded sadly and looked elsewhere for a moment, and she squeezed his hand, and he managed to meet her gaze again for a moment, and a sort of smile passed between them. Another bark.

'And we'll always have Wolf.'

III. A MOMENT IN YOUR LIFE

Just a few hours before, as the wee hours of Friday were crawling towards Saturday morning, Colleen and Wolf had sat up late drinking whisky in his shed (or recording studio, as she had to come to think of it). For the first few minutes they heard Andrew pedantically packing up the car ahead of their departure. Bags were pointedly dragged across gravel and the boot slammed a quite unnecessary number of times. But eventually the sighs and scrapings and slamming ceased, and with the telepathy of twenty-seven years Colleen sensed her husband standing out by the car still, looking around for her across the gravel, gazing forlornly in the direction of the shed but not daring to approach.

'Ach, it's not so difficult to explain,' said Wolf. 'But it is difficult to say.'

'What is?'

'My actual truth.' Wolf paused.

Colleen snorted. 'Oh, this'll be good.' But he silenced her with a look she hadn't seen before.

'Some years ago . . .' He paused again, perhaps for dramatic effect (this was Wolf after all). 'It was after the war. Our parents were dead. My sister and I were brought over here, and . . .'

He stopped. A large tear had formed at the tip of his nose. Colleen had an urge to put her hand on his arm, but she held back. Jack sat still between his master's legs, his big head resting on a knee and his dark poignant eyes staring mournfully at Wolf's.

'We were separated.'

'Separated?'

'They put us in different families, in different parts of the country. I was lucky, my family were kind enough. Correct. Even if there was no place for the likes of me in a land like this.'

'And Hildy?'

'She was not so lucky. The experience . . . undid her.'

'I'm so sorry.'

His shoulders began to heave, and painful sobs shook his frame.

'She spoke no English, she'd lost all her family. *She was only seven years old.*'

'Wolf, that's awful.'

'Ja. But I was there. I could have stopped them separating us. She relied on me.'

'But Wolf, you were only a child yourself.'

'I wanted to go it alone. I was sick of having to look after her. Always moaning and mewling. I wanted to be shot of her.'

'But you were too young to be allowed to make a decision like that.'

'I wanted to be *shot of her*!' he repeated angrily, as if this was a point that had been established so far beyond doubt that no one had any right to question it again.

'I'm sorry,' she said simply.

'You only know for sure when it's too late,' he said, ignoring her. 'You realise later there is a moment in your life, and everything else you are or do will be judged in the light of that moment. And I failed.'

'But surely—'

'One knows. *I know.* I could have done more. My twin sister, my own better self! I should have *died* trying to keep us together! Cometh the hour, cometh . . .' His voice faltered. 'Cometh a *coward.*'

'You're *twins*?'

'Of course. Did I not say?'

'I'm so sorry. So . . . what happened to her? Your sister, I mean?'

'Well, Hildy has survived. In her way. As you can see. But her foster parents were not happy or kind people. To this day she has never told me what really happened. But I remember who she was before.'

'And the wheelchair? Is she . . . ?' Colleen didn't want to pry, except of course she did, more than anything.

'Oh, the chair comes and goes. The real hurt is in her mind. In her soul.'

'I'm so sorry.'

'All I can do now is try to look after her. Try to give her what she wants. A little happiness, on her terms.'

'Yes, I see. And . . . What does she want?'

Wolf topped them up, and stared out into the dark for a long moment.

'Stories,' he said at last. 'She likes . . . *stories.*'

'Stories.'

'Yes.'

Colleen thought she was beginning to understand. 'Like . . . the stories of the people who come to stay here?'

'Yes.'

'Stories . . . like ours.'

'Yes. But the problem is that Hildy is not reasonable!' he shouted, banging the table in exasperation.

'Not . . . reasonable?' replied Colleen dumbly.

'She demands *more*! More detail, more plot, more . . . *drama.*' For a moment he looked almost sheepish. '*More sex.*'

'Wait. So—'

'So if the story is dragging, then is there sometimes a need to . . . give the characters a little nudge or two.' He smiled, as if to himself.

They sat on together, sipping their drams in silence, alone with their thoughts in the harsh glare of the shed's electric light. Darkness was pushing in on them from all sides.

'*Folie a deux*,' said Wolf slowly at last. 'It sounds like such a pretty thing. When I was younger, I thought it was a type of flower. Ha!'

Colleen said with a start, 'And Andrew? Did Andrew know you were doing all this?'

'Not exactly, poor fool. But he knew something was up. I'm afraid we did mess around with his head a little.'

Colleen felt a sharp stab of indignation. She stood up, angry at last. 'So our confusion . . . is Hildy's entertainment? Our *torment* is . . . your penance?'

Wolf's face darkened alarmingly. 'Ach, don't pretend you know about torment! Your generation has seen nothing. You know only things that can be fixed.'

Colleen stared at him as he stood up sharply, almost angry himself, and she was aware again of the incredible vitality of this older man. She wanted to punch him in his stupid grinning mouth. She looked around for something to throw. But there were tears still in his eyes. She didn't know how it happened, but she found herself hugging him. He responded with a stiff hand placed lightly in the middle of her back.

They came apart, and there followed a long silence.

'So, what can we do?' she said at last, briskly switching into work mode for want of any other clue as to what to say or do next.

'What can *you* do?' he snorted quietly. 'Pray that you are never put to the test.'

'You don't think I've been put to the test? Surely you of all people know—'

He held up a hand to cut her short. He stood up, walked over to a workbench. He returned with a laptop, flipped open the screen, hit a couple of buttons.

'Hi, Mum,' said a fuzzy male voice. 'I hear you're in a bit of a fix.'

The moving image was badly delayed and pixel-scarred, but it was unmistakable. She crumpled.

'Don't tell Andrew,' warned Wolf as he let in a small back cat and closed the door behind him, leaving her weeping and laughing at the screen.

IV. ALL PART OF THE HOLIDAY FUN

Late Saturday morning: the hour of departure. Andrew sat behind the wheel, Colleen next to him; he wound down the car window as a familiar figure strode towards them across the gravel.

'So, Wolf, it looks like this is goodbye.'

'Goodbye, sir! Goodbye, my lady! Jack and I will miss you very much. Won't we, old boy?' The older man whistled and patted his wolf, who was frenziedly circling the car and trying to stand on two legs next to his master, clearly aware that some important moment was taking place.

'Hildy sends you all her love too.' Wolf beamed. 'She *so* enjoyed your company, Colleen! Look – there she is now!' Andrew and Colleen looked up to see Hildy waving at them regally from an upstairs window. Her face was swathed in a chignon scarf, from which a few rollers peeped, and her lips were painted in a thick livid fuchsia. She was holding a loofah in a way that even at this distance managed to look obscene.

'We should really report you,' said Andrew so Colleen could hear him. 'What you're doing here . . .'

Wolf took a dramatic step back and clutched his heart. My dear sir!' he began. 'If I thought for one moment that—'

Colleen cut him off. 'I don't think that will be necessary, Andrew, really, do you?' She shot the man she had married a micro-glance that he understood instantly. It said: 'Trust me on this'.

He turned to other matters. 'I'm very sorry, Wolf, but we may have broken a few glasses and things over the course of our stay. I've done my best to tidy everything up, but of course if you can let me know the damage, we'll reimburse you.'

'Think nothing of it, old boy!' cried Wolf. 'I wouldn't dream of it! Natural wear and tear – all part of the holiday fun . . .'

There was a pause.

'Hildy makes an exceptional lasagne,' said Colleen blandly from the passenger seat. 'She's even given me the recipe.'

'She shared it!' hammed Wolf, throwing his hands on his head in mock despair. 'Mein Gott! Guard it with your lives! If that falls into the wrong hands, she'll never forgive me!'

Andrew looked straight ahead. The car started first time.

'Don't worry,' said Colleen. 'Your secret's safe with us.'

'Goodbye, my dears,' twinkled Wolf, and pushed the passenger door closed. 'Yours too.'

V. OPEN

And then last night had happened, and it was she who had cracked wide open.

Ned. Her son. Talking to her on the screen.

She thought of his grainy, Skype-lagged face.

Hi, Mum. I hear you're in a bit of a fix.

She did not want to think about how Wolf had managed to set this call up, not just now.

Ned, oh, Ned. My little boy.

Ned. My son, my broken heart.

My hope.

EPILOGUE

About two hours and fifteen minutes after the departure of Colleen and Andrew, a hired Fiat Uno pulled wearily into the drive. As it came to a halt, the underside of the car caught on a ridge of unseen concrete and made a worrying scraping sound.

A sprightly older gentleman emerged from his attractive Victorian pile to greet the newcomer.

'Good day, sir! Good day! And you must be Gerry!'

The driver of the Fiat Uno, who had lowered his window in order to respond to this wonderfully cheery soul, expressed glad surprise that his name was known.

'Oh, do come in and have a cup of tea! Don't stand on ceremony, sir! Come and meet Hildy! You've just missed Colleen but I believe she had a message for you. Now I'm only a man, of course – but my Hildy knows all the ins and outs . . . *Journeys end in lovers meeting*, and all that! Come in, come in!'

Gerry emerged from the car. His clothes were crumpled from long hours of travel, but their expensive, flamboyant flavour was irrepressible. He wore red denim jeans and cowboy boots, and he carried a battered Tom Ford leather holdall. A small bevvy of colourful ethnic bracelets coiled themselves artfully around one wrist.

He vaped thoughtfully, as he arched his back, putting his frame through a few simple yoga and Pilates moves designed to help refresh mind and body after a long journey. Looking at him from behind, you sensed that the outgrowth of a new ponytail was always a real threat.

The older man, who introduced himself as Wolf, said he believed that Colleen had gone to drop off Andrew somewhere, and was returning here alone to see him. She had booked the cottage for another week. Gerry was more than welcome to stay on as appropriate.

In the meantime, Wolf said, he had heard a nasty rattling coming from Gerry's engine, and he offered to investigate.

ACKNOWLEDGEMENTS

A huge thank you to everyone who has helped make this book happen.

To Alex, John and Martin, who gave invaluable feedback and suggestions on my original idea. To all the other members of my writer's group too – especially Christy, Debs, Maire, Tom and Nandarane – for all your ideas and encouragement.

To my first readers Jenny Fielder, Mary Mackenzie, Eve Brotzel, Sarah Riley and of course David Bliss. To Fr Mark Drew, special linguistic pedantry consultant (remaining errors mine). Thank you for all your feedback.

To Lloyd Cole, for his kind permission to quote from one of his lyrics.

To Moira and Bob at Sandstone, for taking me on. To Moira too, for culling many unnecessary adverbs and making this a far better book with her patient edits. To Anna Paterson for her painstaking proofreading, and Nathan Burton for his witty cover.

To Ger, for all your constant support and encouragement.

To Rob Pointer, my oldest and blondest friend, who has 'been with me since the beginning'. Thank you for always believing in me, old boy.